ISBN: 978-1-950902-65-1

A SABOTAGED CELEBRATION
AND SALMON SNAPS

ALEKSA BAXTER

CHAPTER ONE

IT WAS A THURSDAY MORNING AT ELEVEN AND I WAS STILL in the same pajamas and sweatshirt I'd worn the day before and I honestly did not care. They were comfortable and when you have absolutely no reason to change into "real" clothes, pajamas are the best clothing option out there in my humble opinion.

They don't pinch. They're soft. And they don't point out to you that you've probably gained five pounds since you stopped working in a real job by digging into your belly. In other words, I think we should all wear pajamas all the time and we'd be much happier.

But, alas, that is not the world most of us live in.

Fortunately for me, at that point my world consisted of my dog, Fancy, who was a three-year-old Newfoundland and perfectly fine with me no matter what I wore, my grandpa, who had run away to Las Vegas to spend a drama-free few days with his new love before Christmas, and my boyfriend, Matt, who had run down to Denver with some friends to see the Avs game, do some shopping, and pick up my grandpa and Lesley from the airport.

Which meant I, at least, could get away with pajamas as non-stop daywear. It's also why I wasn't too concerned with the stain or two on my sweatshirt from trying to eat fruit cups without a spoon. (They work a lot like bottles of ketchup. Nothing's coming out and then suddenly all of it wants to come out at once.)

Anyway.

Since the closing of the barkery I had discovered that at heart I was really a slob, something I'd never known before since I'd been working or in school since I was fourteen-years-old. It turns out those twenty-two years of hard work and accomplishment weren't because I was inherently motivated, they were instead just a product of others' expectations and a failure to question my own direction.

But with the barkery closed and nothing better to do but read books, invent dog treats, and develop an addiction to computer games, I'd found my true happy state.

One little problem. Fancy was not on board with my newfound slothfulness. As she made very clear, standing in the doorway, yipping at me to get off my butt and go outside with her.

"Fancy. It's snowy outside. And it's cold. I don't like snow. Or cold."

She barked—one loud, short demand for attention.

"Fancy…Ten minutes. Okay? I promise."

She plopped down in the doorway and gave me that look she has that says she'll lay there and be quiet because she knows she has no other choice, but that she's very broken-hearted and disappointed by her horrible, awful mother who won't even come out and play in the snow with her.

If I'd had something meaningful I was doing—like campaigning for world peace—I would've felt better about ignoring her. But since all I was doing was trying very hard to place in the top five of that day's solitaire tournament, I felt horribly guilty.

Not guilty enough to stop, though. The way those stupid tournaments were set up if I stopped it might just keep on counting time against me. And it certainly wouldn't let me continue that particular game where I'd left off. I'd have to start all over again and I was not going to do that on an expert-level Spider that I'd already spent five minutes on.

Fancy whined so softly it was practically subsonic. I spared her a quick glare because I knew she would do that for a half hour straight if she was so inclined, which she clearly was.

"Give me a break, Fancy. It's cold out."

That was the one part of living in a small town in the Colorado mountains that I hadn't given quite enough thought to. The winters. That came with snow. And freezing temperatures.

Oh sure, I was aware that's what happened in Colorado in the wintertime and especially in the mountains. But I'd had some naïve notion that a town situated at seven thousand feet was somehow going to have a winter like Denver where it snowed on Monday but everything had melted and it was back to fifty degrees Fahrenheit by Wednesday most of the time.

That was not the case.

Fancy whined again, staring me down with those sad amber eyes of hers.

"Fine." She jumped to her feet. "But. I have to finish this game first." She dropped back down to the ground with a loud huff.

I was sorry to disappoint her, but I did have to finish. Didn't I? I mean, this was about proving the kind of person

I am. And I am the type of person who finishes what I start, even when it is a meaningless computer game.

Fancy obviously didn't think so. She flopped onto her side with a gusty sigh.

"Almost there. I promise. Just one more stack…"

I growled at the screen. All I needed was a seven of spades. How hard was that?

Fancy huffed at me again and then stood up and left.

"Fancy…I'm sorry, but…"

I turned my attention back to the screen. Almost there…

It took another two minutes which pretty much destroyed my chances of placing in the top ten for the day. (Top ten of my measly little group of a hundred out of three hundred thousand, but let's not go there.)

At that point I figured I might as well stop and go walk Fancy because even if they did add on time to my game it wasn't going to change things enough to matter.

Fancy was ecstatic when I came out into the living room. She ran around with her favorite zippo hippo dangling from her mouth as I layered on enough clothes to survive the arctic chill outside.

(Not that I know that it was technically an arctic chill in Colorado. But it's one of those things you say and then some goodie goodie comes along and tells you you're wrong and spends five minutes of your life you'll never get back explaining to you the real word you should've used when it honestly doesn't even matter. Can you tell I've been spending a little too much time around Lesley's library friends who know *everything* and insist on correcting anyone who gets any little thing wrong? Actually, I think I was that way when I was a kid. Might be why people didn't always like to be around me.)

Anyway.

By the time I'd added a sweatshirt to my long-sleeved shirt and then a winter jacket and scarf on top of that, Fancy was raring to go. She'd already run five laps of the living room and finally settled for standing in front of the door like a statue, just waiting, waiting, waiting like that old Mervyn's commercial with the lady saying open, open, open.

I leashed her up which was the point where she'd normally drop her toy, but not this time. She was taking it with us. A sign that she was truly desperately in need of some attention.

I opened the door onto the part of Colorado I don't like. The cold part. The icy part. The part that unfortunately exists in the mountains for a good chunk of the year.

I'd seriously underestimated the amount of days that could involve snow falling out of the sky or crowding up the streets when I'd made my decision to move to Creek to take care of my grandpa.

(A man who it turned out did not need my care.)

Left to my own devices, I would've hibernated for the entire winter, not leaving the house except for when I had to buy groceries. But weather like this was Fancy's happy place. The more it snowed, the more she wanted to be outside. Preferably with me in tow.

So as I miserably trudged through the snow, Fancy frisked along like a puppy, head held high, her little tail swishing back and forth, her bright blue toy dangling from her mouth as she looked for fun and adventure.

Newfies, I tell ya. I think they live in an alternate world where snow is actually a white sand beach and blizzard-level winds are just a pleasant breeze.

At least it wasn't nostril-freezing cold out...

But it was close.

Which is why I shuffled her around the block and back home within about ten minutes of our leaving. I loved her. And I knew she loved to be outside in that kind of weather. But she had a backyard now. She didn't need me out there freezing to death keeping her company.

Love. It has to have some limits, doesn't it?

CHAPTER TWO

I'D JUST REMOVED ALL OF THE LAYERS OF CLOTHING AND snuggled myself up for the last game of the solitaire tournament when my phone started ringing.

I not-so-silently cussed at it. Probably some solicitor trying to scam me out of my hard-earned money.

I'd been receiving calls lately from some woman who left these complicated voicemails about this horrible thing that was happening to her that sounded like a wrong number. I'd almost called her back the first time because she was so good at it, but then she called again with some completely different sob story and I realized what was happening.

She wasn't being sexually harassed at work or about to get evicted from her apartment or desperately trying to reach her cousin because his aunt was in the hospital and on the verge of death. She just wanted me to call her back so she could somehow scam me.

Just in case it was someone I'd actually want to talk to (unlikely but possible), I glanced at the phone, losing two precious seconds from my game time, and cussed again.

It was Mason Maxwell, fiancé of my best friend Jamie whose wedding was only nine days away. I sighed.

Mason was not exactly someone I wanted to talk to—he's a bit uptight for my tastes—but I had to. Jamie had been too fragile since the whole Ted Little affair and I couldn't afford to ignore it if Mason was calling for my help.

I know. You're thinking to yourself, what Ted Little affair? I don't remember her telling me about that.

And you're right. I didn't. For two reasons. First, there was nothing funny or entertaining about what happened with Ted Little. That man was truly evil and he almost took away my best friend. Second, because I was just a helpless observer who didn't do anything useful to bring him down, so my part of the story would have been really boring.

But since you should probably know what happened, let me give you a quick recap.

I ran into Ted Little when I was looking for Trish, Sam's mom, after she went missing. (I did tell you about that.) He really scared me the first time I met him even though I was with Matt. But he scared me even more when he came walking into the barkery one day when I was all alone even though he didn't own a dog.

Matt and my grandpa insisted that I not give him any chance to get at me since he'd been suspected in the disappearance of three women before he went to prison for burning some guy's house down. So when he showed up, I called Matt and let him know. And I kept doing so until Ted Little finally backed off.

I thought that was the end of it. But it turns out that when he couldn't get me alone, he focused in on Jamie instead. And before any of us realized what had happened, she was missing.

If it hadn't been for a very strange woman who was

passing through town—she talked to herself a lot but it was like she was having actual conversations with other people, multiple other people—we might not have found Jamie at all.

Fortunately, Mason and Matt were desperate enough they followed the crazy woman when she led them down some remote mountain road to a cabin tucked away where no one even knew it existed.

And they found Jamie. *Before* Ted Little had a chance to do anything serious. (They also found the bodies of five other women, so we know what *would* have happened. That strange woman saved Jamie from…a lot.)

Like I said, nothing funny or entertaining about it. And I wasn't even there. So not my story to tell. Maybe Ruby will write about it someday. (That's the crazy woman. According to Matt she found Jamie because she followed the ghost of one of Ted Little's other victims. Yeah, right. Like ghosts really exist.)

Anyway. Scary situation. But all over. Everyone safe. Ted Little back in prison.

Unfortunately, Jamie's way of coping was to move the wedding date up to New Year's Eve and insist on doing everything herself. Two hundred guests and she wanted to not only plan and coordinate the whole thing but make all of the food, too.

Fortunately, I'd talked her out of making the five-course sit-down meal, but she'd still insisted on making the wedding cupcakes. And some sort of hand-made party favors that I didn't even want to know about.

If it was anyone but Jamie I would've sat her down and said, "Don't you even think about it." But this was Jamie and Jamie is Wonder Woman. She can do anything she sets her mind to. So I just stepped aside and let her go.

(I did offer to help, before you think too poorly of me, but Jamie knows how much I hate weddings so she told me it was fine. Everything was fine. I knew she was probably lying, but you only push people so far, you know?)

But if Mason was calling...

Well, that was a bad sign. So yet again I closed out of my tournament.

"Hey, Mason. What's up?" I said.

"Maggie. We have a problem."

"With the wedding?" I grimaced. I really do hate weddings. I'd go, because Jamie was my best friend, but until the day of I was trying to ignore the fact that this big awful social event was hurtling my way. So many awkward conversations...Ugh.

"With the wedding dress, actually. It just arrived."

"And?" I asked, showing great restraint in not demanding to know why was he calling me and ruining my chance to win my solitaire tournament over a wedding dress.

He sighed. A very un-Mason-like sound. "From what I can gather between sobs, it is the wrong size."

"So you get a seamstress to fix it, right?"

"I suggested that..."

"Didn't go over well?"

"No. Something about custom beading and seams that I did not understand. Maggie, I have never seen Jamie cry. And I do not know how to get her to stop."

"Well, for what it's worth, I've only seen her cry once. And I'm not sure I was much help getting her to stop then. But I'll come over and see what I can do."

"Thank you."

As I bundled up yet again, I shook my head. The things we do for friends...

CHAPTER THREE

FANCY WAS NOT HAPPY WHEN I LEFT HER AT HOME. BUT I figured she'd never been to Mason's house before and a crisis was not the time to introduce a hundred-and-forty-pound dog who liked to be muddy into the house of a man who was best described as fastidious.

And, wow, what a house it was. *All* wood and stone.

It wasn't as fancy as Greta's house—that was a flat-out mansion meant to impress—but it was definitely memorable. Three stories of what could best be described as "rugged mountain chic". There was a lot of wood that you knew was absolutely not hand-carved like it appeared to be.

And lots of artful use of river stone. There were beds of stone along the driveway and stone incorporated into the façade as well. It was like someone wanted to say, "I may be rich but I am also a part of these here mountains."

It was…interesting. Tasteful even. For what it was.

But once again I found myself contemplating the odd fact that so many people I knew had found happiness with someone I would not have lasted through a first date with.

Mason had turned out to be a decent guy and I liked how he was with Jamie, but...yeah, not my type.

I didn't even reach the front door before he yanked it open. "Maggie. So glad you're here."

He was in what I figured most rich men wear when lounging around their mountain homes. Black slacks, a soft black sweater that was probably cashmere, and black shoes that weren't slippers but clearly weren't outdoor shoes either. It all fit very well with his salt and pepper hair and rugged good looks.

"Is she still crying?" I stepped inside, wondering if this was the type of home where outdoor shoes weren't allowed and, if so, what Mason would think of my socks that had little Newfie heads on them and were bright pink.

"Worse. She's in my office looking up flights."

He nodded to a shoe rack off to the side of the entryway and I reluctantly removed my shoes and then had to bite my lip when he handed me my very own pair of house shoes. Well, at least I wouldn't slip and fall on the spiral staircase made of more wood and stone.

There was that, at least.

"Flights to where? Does she want to elope?" I asked as I put on the surprisingly comfortable shoes.

"No. The wedding is still on. But she wants to go to New York."

"New York? Why?"

"She wants to find the wedding designer and have them fix the dress."

"I take it they're in New York?"

"That is the return address on the box the dress came in. But I don't know if that is really where the designer is located."

I nodded. "Got it." Clearly Jamie had entered full-on crazy mode where rational thought no longer existed.

I took a deep breath, preparing myself to handle something I'd never had to deal with before—my best friend in panic mode—and turned to Mason. "Where's your office?"

Mason visibly relaxed as he pointed me up the stairs and down a hallway paved with larger stones I was just sure would be Colorado-sourced.

Give me carpet any day. It's a lot more comfortable on bare feet. (Not that I could picture Mason walking around barefoot, ever. He probably wore shoes in the shower. But still.)

I found the office easily enough. It continued the theme of high-end mountain man with its deep rich browns and greens and leather, not to mention a desk that looked to have been custom-made from a large slab of wood. (Bet that didn't come from Colorado, though. We have tall trees, but I don't think we have trees that big around. Probably a California redwood or something like that.)

I paused in the doorway to study Jamie.

She's normally so put together with her brown hair styled perfectly and a touch of makeup and color-coordinated outfits. But that day…

Her hair was a greasy, ratted mess and if the circles under her eyes were any indication she wasn't sleeping and hadn't bothered with makeup. And the clothes she'd chosen were…clothes. I'll give her that.

They weren't pajamas, so she hadn't sunk to my level. Yet. But they definitely weren't Jamie clothes.

I wondered where she'd even found them since I didn't expect her closet or Mason's had such a shabby selection. No wonder Mason was concerned.

"Hey Jamie," I called, putting as much forced cheer into my voice as I could manage.

"Oh, hey Maggie. What are you doing here?" She barely looked away from the laptop to greet me.

"Just wanted to stop by and see how things are going." I dropped into the brown leather chair across from the desk. "So…How are things going? Everything on track? You finalize the menu with the caterer?"

I figured I'd ease into the whole wedding dress issue, but that backfired, big time.

She stared at me, eyes wide with panic. "The caterer. I'm supposed to meet with him at one to go over the final details. What time is it?" She glanced at the computer. "It's already noon. He's in Bakerstown. I can…" She stood and then froze like her mind had overloaded. "I need…But I have to…"

"Sit."

She obeyed me, eyes still too wide for normal.

"Do you have the caterer's number?"

She nodded.

"Okay. Good. Give it to me. I'll call him. We'll reschedule for tomorrow."

She shook her head. "But I'll be in New York by tomorrow. My dress…I have to…"

"No. You will not be in New York tomorrow."

"But I have to go. The dress was the wrong size. I have to fix it."

"Yeah, well, you're not going to fix it by going to New York. Did you book a ticket yet?"

"No. I was just about to…" She turned back towards the laptop.

"Don't. Close that computer down. Now."

"But…"

"Close it."

She closed the laptop.

"Good. Now where is your room?"

"Down the hall."

"Okay. Let's go." I stood and waited for her.

She stood up, looking very confused. "Where?"

"To get you cleaned up."

She looked around again, lost. "But...There's so much to do. I can't..."

"It will wait until after you brush your hair and take a shower. Trust me."

I wasn't one to talk since I'd been lounging around at home for the last couple days without bothering to shower myself, but she needed it. Badly. This was not the Jamie I knew. She needed to get back to her old self and then we could tackle this whole issue of the messed-up wedding dress.

CHAPTER FOUR

While Jamie took a shower, I dug up the caterer's number from her collection of five three-ring wedding binders that were neatly arranged on a small desk in the sitting area of the ginormous bedroom she shared with Mason. (Honestly, I think that bedroom was bigger than some people's houses.)

The binders took planning and organization to an entirely new level. There were tabs and spreadsheets and sample products and who knew what else in there. She could've probably sold the system for thousands of dollars it was so amazingly cross-referenced and detailed.

And right there under the caterer tab was the number of The Baker Valley Catering Company. (The only independent catering company in the valley. Fortunately, they made truly excellent food.)

That section included a detailed menu with Jamie's notes about what she'd chosen as well as a listing of all known food allergies and food preferences from the RSVPs, cross-indexed to where each individual was going to be seated. She'd gone so far as to put all of the nut allergies at their own table as well as all of the vegans together at another table.

It was...something, alright.

(Me, I would've honored the allergies because you don't want anyone dying at your wedding, but I would not have paid for ten different menu selections just to honor people's food preferences. Vegetarian or vegan is fine enough, but some of the preferences she'd received back? Oh hell no. You want to be that particular, honey, you find your own meal.)

Anyway.

I dialed the number and when a woman answered on the second ring I asked for James, the head caterer.

He picked up a moment later. "James Kingston."

"James. It's Maggie from the Baker Valley Barkery and Café. How are you?"

"Good, Maggie. To what do I owe the pleasure?"

"Well, I know Jamie had a meeting scheduled with you at one to finalize the menu, but is there any way to move that to tomorrow? She's a bit frazzled at the moment. A wedding dress snafu has thrown her for a loop."

There was a long pause on the other end of the line.

"James?"

"Um, Maggie, we're not catering Jamie's wedding."

"But you're right here in her wedding binder. Who else would be doing it if it isn't you guys?"

"I don't know. That's why I was so surprised when she cancelled on us a week ago."

"She cancelled on you?"

"Yep. Sent an email. Said she'd decided to do it herself and sorry for the late notice. Offered to pay the full cost of any supplies we'd already bought."

I glanced towards the bathroom door where I could hear

Jamie singing in the shower. "Jamie would never do something like that via email. Are you sure?"

"Positive. I've got the email right here."

"Can you send that email to me?" I rattled off my email address for him.

"Sure. Give me a minute."

I made my way back to the office and opened up Jamie's laptop so I could access my email. A few seconds later the email arrived. At first glance it did look like Jamie's email—it had the right name on it—but when I looked closer I realized that the email address had a period between the first and last names and Jamie's real email address doesn't.

"Huh. That's interesting," I said.

"What? What is it?"

"This email didn't come from Jamie. The address is wrong."

Another long silence on the other end of the line.

"James…Any chance you can still do the wedding?"

I knew the answer before he gave it.

"I'm sorry, Maggie. We booked up immediately afterwards with another event. I can't do both."

"But she didn't *really* cancel on you, you know."

"I know. But…"

"Is there anyone else that you can think of that could handle it?"

"Not anyone local, that's for sure. I was gonna be stretched to the limit trying to do it myself."

I stared at the bookcase in Mason's office that had a whole set of books on procedural law that looked like they'd make good paperweights but poor reading. "And you probably cancelled all of the ingredient orders already?"

"Yeah, I did. And some of that stuff…No way to get it all in now."

"Okay. Thanks."

"Sorry, Maggie, I...I wish I could help."

"So do I." I hung up and stared out the window for a long, long moment. What were the odds that both the wedding dress and the caterer were messed up and nothing else was?

I did not have a good feeling about this.

CHAPTER FIVE

WHEN I WALKED BACK TO THE BEDROOM I COULD HEAR
Jamie singing *Joy to the World* through the bathroom door.
(Not the Christmas song. The 70's classic by Three Dog
Night.) Fortunately, she has a much better voice than I do.

As I listened to how happy she was I realized there was
no way I could tell her about the caterer. Not after the dress
fiasco.

She came out of the bathroom with more Jamie-like
clothes on and a big smile on her face. "Oh, that felt so
good. I needed that. Thank you."

She gave me a quick hug and I hugged her back,
wincing inwardly at what I was going to have to do.

She glanced at the wedding binders. "Were you able to
reschedule with James? When do I have to meet with him?"

I took a deep, painful breath. Friendship. Sometimes it
requires sacrifice. "Actually, you don't."

"What? Why not?"

"Because I'm going to take care of it. All of it."

"But, no. It's my wedding. I wanted to plan it."

"And you have. Look at these binders. They are a

miracle of hard-work and planning. But you're the bride, Jamie. You can't work yourself into the ground before your big day. Take the time between now and the wedding, book a spa appointment, run away for a few days with Mason, catch up on some reading...Just relax."

She shook her head. "No. Maggie, I can't just sit around. I can't. I'll...No."

But she couldn't keep planning this wedding. Not if what I suspected had happened, had happened.

"I'll tell ya what. You keep the cupcakes. And whatever fancy party favor you're doing. I'll take the rest." I forced my best smile. "I have the binders. I know what you want, I know what you've set up, and I will make sure this goes off without a hitch. I'll even figure out the wedding dress situation."

"You're sure?"

"Absolutely. You only get married once, right?" (One would hope and one will certainly pretend while preparing for a friend's first wedding.) "Let me help you make this the best day ever."

I continued to smile even as my gut clenched in dread.

"Oh, Maggie. Thank you!" Jamie threw her arms around me, clutching at me more than hugging me. "It's... Everything has been so awful lately, and...I thought working on the wedding would help, but...Oh, thank you. You don't know what this means to me."

I patted her awkwardly on the back. "You're welcome. That's what friends are for, right?"

She nodded as I pulled away from her. "I owe you. When you and Matt get married..."

"Whoa, there. Don't go talking crazy. Matt's great and I really love him...But...No. No, no, no. Just, no."

I did love Matt. And I couldn't imagine being with

someone else or not being with him. But, marriage? I was just getting used to the idea of having an actual plus one for a wedding for the first time in my life. That would be plenty for me for the next, say, five years?

I patted the stack of binders. "Now. I do need one thing from you. I need you to look through these binders and make sure they're completely up to date so that I have all of the information I need to make this come off perfectly."

"Okay. Sure. I can do that." She smiled and was the old happy Jamie. That alone made the hell the next week of my life was about to become all worthwhile.

"Great. While you're doing that, I'm just going to run downstairs real quick and tell Mason about the change in plans and find myself a Coke. Okay?"

"Okay! There should be a few Cokes in the main fridge. I bought them just for you."

Somehow I managed to keep the fake smile on my face all the way out of the room. And then I ran.

CHAPTER SIX

I FOUND MASON IN THE "KITCHEN"—AN EXPANSE OF space with even more wood and more stone, two ovens, two fridges, and a mini fridge. (What single man has two ovens in his house? Seriously.)

"Mason."

He spun around at my tone of voice. "What? What is it? Is Jamie okay?"

I glanced around, making sure Jamie hadn't followed me into the kitchen. "Jamie's fine, but we have a problem. A big one. I think someone is trying to sabotage your wedding."

He laughed. "Because of a wedding dress? Don't be ridiculous."

"It's not just the wedding dress. Someone emailed the caterer pretending to be Jamie and cancelled. He already took on a new client for that night."

"But we have two hundred guests coming."

"I know. And let's hope that you still have a venue and flowers and a pastor and whatever else goes into a wedding. Not to mention the guests."

I'd never seen Mason lost for words before, but he just stared at me and then finally said, "Why wouldn't we?"

"Because if someone cancelled the caterer and sent the wrong measurements to the dress manufacturer, what else might they have done?"

He paled. "Who would do something like that?"

"I don't know. That's what we need to find out. Do you have any exes or enemies that might do something like this?"

He rubbed his hands through his hair, the most nervous I'd ever seen him look. "I might have one."

"Really? An ex or an enemy?"

"An ex. We, um, we were engaged." He rubbed the back of his neck. "And I broke it off."

I hadn't heard about this. "When?"

He licked his lips and wouldn't meet my eyes.

"When did you break off this engagement, Mason?"

"The first time I saw Jamie."

"You broke off an engagement to ask my friend out?" I had to struggle to keep my voice down.

"No. It wasn't like that. I..." He paced away from me and then back. "I saw Jamie when she came in to sign the lease for the barkery. It was about a year ago. We didn't even speak. I just..." He shook his head. "I saw her and I realized that if I could feel that kind of spark for a woman I didn't know that I should not be marrying Elaine. That it was not fair to her for me to do that. So I broke it off. It was months before Jamie and I actually went on our first date."

"Does Jamie know about this?"

He shook his head. "No. It never came up."

"It never came up that you were engaged less than a year ago? How does that not come up?"

"Jamie did not want to know about my exes. She said all

that mattered was the future we were going to make together, not the past. So I didn't ask about hers either."

(That was probably a good thing. Jamie had a lot of exes. A lot.)

I shook my head, marveling at the fact that Jamie and I were such good friends when we were also such polar opposites in so many ways. I couldn't imagine marrying someone not knowing that they'd been engaged before.

If I was getting married I'd want the name of every single girl my future husband had ever kissed as well as a rundown of everything about her and why they hadn't worked out. And then I'd want to talk through each one in detail to make sure that none of those issues were going to be our issues.

(There are reasons I've stayed single so long. Many, many reasons.)

I put on my best interrogator's face. "Have you been *married* before?"

"No."

"Do you have some random kid hidden away?"

"No. Why would you ask a thing like that?"

"Well, if you were previously engaged who knows what else you're hiding."

Mason pinched the bridge of his nose. "Being engaged is not the same as being married or having a kid."

"I don't know about that. They're all serious life commitments. I mean, whoever this woman was you got down on one knee and asked her to marry you, didn't you? Only difference between that and being married to her is saying some vows in front of an audience."

He huffed out a breath, but before he could say something caustic about my weird perspective on the world, Jamie came into the kitchen to join us, setting down a box overflowing with the wedding binders. "All done. Everything is exactly as it should be."

She gave me a big hug. "Thank you so much for doing this, Maggie. I can't tell you how happy I am that you're helping out with the wedding."

"Of course. What are friends for?" I met Mason's eyes. I hoped Jamie still thought I was amazing when this was all over. Because I had a feeling I was going to be planning a wedding for two hundred people from scratch with only nine days to make it happen. And that was not going to be easy in small-town Colorado in the middle of winter on New Year's Eve.

CHAPTER SEVEN

MASON CARRIED THE BOX OF BINDERS OUT TO MY VAN for me. It was getting colder, the wind whipping around and blowing hints of smoke towards us. (From fireplaces, not forest fires, thankfully.)

He put the box in the back. "I will keep Jamie distracted until the wedding while you figure out how bad it is."

"Sounds good. She's still making all the cupcakes and wedding favors, so that should help. But keep an eye on things there, too. I don't know how close this person is to you guys."

"I want to find them."

"We will. But in the meantime, I suspect we're going to be planning this entire wedding from scratch. So...um... How much do I have to work with money-wise? I assume most of the deposits you guys already made are going to be lost."

"Whatever you need."

"Mason...This could be very expensive. I'm trying to put together a wedding for two hundred people with nine days' notice."

"Like I said. Whatever you need. I love her and there is no amount of money I would not spend to make her happy."

"While that's a nice sentiment, most people's bank accounts and mortgage payments put a practical limit on these things. So at least give me a number that when we hit it I should let you know."

"A hundred thousand."

I coughed. "A hundred thousand. On top of whatever you may have already lost?"

"I told you. She is my world. And that is not the upper limit, Maggie. That is just the number where you should call me and tell me how bad it is going to be."

I shuddered. "I can't imagine spending that much on a single day's event. For that much money you should get gold-plated silverware to take home with you and be carried around on the shoulders of five Sherpas the whole day."

He laughed. "Hardly. You are about to learn just how expensive these kinds of things can get. The meal alone will probably be half of that."

"Not if I can help it."

"Maggie..." He caught my gaze and held it. "This is Jamie's wedding. Give her what she wants. Please."

"Fine. I will do everything in my power and your bank account to give her the wedding she thought she'd already planned."

"Thank you."

I shuddered once more as I got into the car. Why on earth would anyone spend that kind of money on a single day?

Yet more proof that I am simply not wired like a large part of the population. There is nothing about weddings that appeals to me. Not the big party, not the fancy dress, not the ring that catches on your hair for the rest of your life, not wearing white, none of it.

And yet there I was. Planning the social event of the year.

What can I tell you? Life is ironic.

CHAPTER EIGHT

THE FIRST THING I DID WHEN I GOT HOME WAS GIVE Fancy some ear scratches and a handful of Salmon Snaps, my newest and greatest dog treat invention.

What? You thought the first thing I did when I got home was call to see how royally messed up the wedding plans were? Then you've obviously never had an incredibly spoiled dog that's about as big as you are and very demanding of attention when she's been left alone for any period of time.

Only after I'd given Fancy a sufficient amount of hugs and kisses to make up for my absence did I sit down at the kitchen table and start making calls.

First call was to the dress manufacturer. Sure enough. They'd received an email with updated measurements. I asked why they hadn't bothered to call when the measurements were so completely different from the original measurements they'd been given, and was lectured on how "it wasn't their problem, lady, sometimes people gain weight before a wedding", by someone with a very strong Bronx accent.

Who knows? Maybe Jamie could've flown to New York and resolved the issue, but I suspect an in-person conversation would not have gone any better than my phone call did. The dress was a loss. They couldn't and wouldn't make any changes at that point. Didn't I know how long it takes to make a wedding dress? I mean, really, lady, not their problem.

Next was the florist. They too had received an email cancelling the order and couldn't possibly get the baby pink roses that Jamie had wanted in on such short notice.

Good news on the hotel. They still had a reserved room block for the wedding and it was full up with confirmed wedding guests. I made them promise not to cancel any of the reservations without talking to me first.

Bad news on the reception venue. It too had been cancelled via email with no way to rebook. I asked why someone hadn't asked Jamie about it, or Mason about it. I mean, this was a small enough community they had to have crossed paths with one or the other of the two since the email was sent.

I was told that no one wanted to risk offending Mason's family by appearing to be ungrateful so they'd just sucked it up and kept silent.

(Although it was very clear there had been some private conversations about the type of bride who books a wedding with only a month's notice and then turns around two weeks later and cancels all of her arrangements. It seems Jamie, Mason, and I were probably the only ones involved with the wedding who hadn't known about all of the cancellations.)

At least we still had a pastor and a church. I warned him not to pay attention to any emails he might receive from Jamie, Mason, or anyone else, including me, because the only way his participation in the event was going to be cancelled was if I showed up in person to do so.

After that call I put my head down on the table and let myself have a minor breakdown.

It could've been worse. We had a pastor and guests at least. And those guests had somewhere to stay while they were in town. I wasn't going to have to ask them to couch surf or stay in a heated barn or anything. So there was that.

But I still needed somewhere to have the reception. And food to feed everyone. All *two hundred* of them.

And a wedding dress, of course.

Not to mention I needed to figure out who had done this to Jamie. Because if I didn't figure that out there was a good chance they'd keep trying to sabotage the wedding and then I or Mason might end up doing something regrettable that would *really* ruin the wedding.

But before I could do any of that...

I glanced at the clock.

Matt, his brother Jack, my grandpa, and Lesley were due back from Denver in half an hour and I hadn't even bothered to set the table yet. At least I'd put a chicken bacon potato spinach soup in the slow cooker that morning so there'd be food to eat.

(One of the problems of living in a really small town is you can't just run out and grab something for dinner at the local fast food restaurant or pizza joint. You have to actually prepare for meals. It was an adjustment, especially compared to living in a big city like DC.)

I gathered up the five lovely three-ring binders and put them aside. Nothing more I could do on the wedding front until the morning, but that wasn't going to stop me from worrying about how to pull this all off with less than ten days to go and Christmas smack dab in the middle of that.

CHAPTER NINE

IT WAS A GOOD THING I'D ALREADY DECIDED TO PUT THE wedding disaster aside until the next day, because my grandpa and Lesley threw me for such a loop that night that I was pretty much useless for anything but staring at them with my mouth wide open.

I knew something was up when Matt came in the door first—as tall, dark, and handsome as ever—and immediately pulled me into a big embrace. Not that we don't hug when we see each other—we are a couple after all—but this was one of those "pull you close so I can whisper something important" hugs.

He buried his mouth against my ear and said, "Play it cool, Maggie," before pulling away.

"Play what cool?" I muttered as my grandpa escorted Lesley through the door. They were both glowing and giggling like kids. Which is saying something for a man who's normally taciturn and a woman who is never anything but perfectly put together.

"Guess what?" My grandpa took off his coat and I saw

that he was wearing nice slacks and a sweater rather than his standard jeans and flannel shirt.

"What?" I asked, knowing already I didn't actually want to know.

Lesley held up her left hand and flashed a wedding ring. "We got married!"

I couldn't breathe for a second, but I forced a smile.

"Congratulations!" I hugged them both, looking at Matt with horror eyes over their shoulders.

Wasn't this sudden? It was sudden, wasn't it? It was really sudden. I mean, her husband had just passed away a couple months before. And, sure they'd known each other forever and even dated before Lesley met her husband, but…This was sudden, yeah?

I mean, my grandpa was eighty-two-years-old and Lesley was probably right up around there, but still…

Was I the only one in the world who thought it was a good idea to at least date someone for a year before you married them? I mean, how could you know what you needed to know about them if you didn't at least spend a year with them? What if they disappeared fishing every summer? Or turned into a shouting beast every football season? Or spent the month of January in a depressed stupor?

How could you know you wanted to spend forever with someone you hadn't even spent a year with?

And putting that aside, what did my grandpa getting married mean for me?

I know it was selfish to think, but…

Was Lesley going to move in now? Should I move out? Where would I go? It was way too early to move in with Matt, not to mention he had a more than full house with Jack and Sam and Trish.

It was awkward enough living with my grandpa, but with some strange woman who was always perfectly coiffed and put together? What was that going to be like?

The only good thing about their news—other than their obvious happiness, of course—was the fact that it cleared all thoughts of Jamie's wedding completely out of my mind.

Lesley beamed at me. "I know it's sudden, Maggie. But we're not young either one of us. And we knew we wanted this. So why wait? Who cares what other people think?" She looked at my grandpa with such adoration I didn't even know what to say.

So I made it up. "Hey, I understand. When you find that person you want to be with for the rest of your life…Why wait, right?"

My laugh probably sounded a bit panicked, because Jack, Matt's brother, who'd snuck his way inside and was leaning against the wall watching the whole scene with far too much amusement, said, "Really? Is that how you feel, Maggie? Once you know you've found the one, just get married? Right away?"

I glared daggers at him. He knew me better than that. And Matt did not need to go getting any ideas, thank you very much.

I swallowed my panic. "Well, when you're the age my grandpa and Lesley are, and you've known each other as long as they have…Sure. Why not?"

Matt kissed my cheek and rubbed the back of my neck. "Don't worry, Maggie. No one's trying to force you into anything crazy like marriage."

I smiled up at him with probably too much relief, but I knew Matt. He was decided already. And all this talk of love and marriage was just going to make him wonder why I wasn't. And, true, I wasn't going to find a better man, ever. But...

Give me a year, would ya?

Ugh.

Lifelong commitments are...well, *lifelong*. I mean, at our age, that was fifty-plus years of your life.

Living with one person. Day in. And day out. Hours a day together...

I'm sorry, but no one is so perfect that you're going to like them while living in close proximity with them for *fifty years*. At least, not if you're me. Heck, there are people I can't stand for five minutes let alone fifty years...

To stop my spiraling desire to sprint for the door and never return, I turned it back on Jack instead. "Speaking of lifelong commitments, Jack. How you and Trish getting on? You headed for the altar anytime soon?"

He winked at me. "As a matter of fact, I'm planning on proposing New Year's Eve. Matt helped me pick out the ring while we were in Denver."

I froze, not daring to look at Matt. Please, please, someone tell me that he hadn't picked up on all of this wedding insanity. I loved him, but if he proposed to me on New Year's Eve...I'd...No. Just, no.

"Aren't you going to be at Jamie's wedding?" I asked.

"I thought that was moved to some other date."

"What? Where did you hear that?"

He shook his head. "I don't know. Someone mentioned it somewhere."

"Oh no." I buried my head against Matt's chest.

"What's wrong, Maggie? What is it?" he asked.

I pulled away. "Let's get the food served up and I'll tell you all what's going on with Jamie's wedding. Because I am going to need some serious help if I'm going to pull this one off."

CHAPTER TEN

RATHER THAN DEALING WITH THE LACK OF A CATERER, lack of a venue, lack of flowers, and lack of wedding dress the next morning, I found myself at the kitchen table with my portion of the guest list making calls to confirm who was coming and who wasn't.

My grandpa, Lesley, and Jack worked their own portions of the list at the same time. (Matt was at work or he'd have helped out, too.)

It turned out whoever our saboteur was, they didn't have the guest list. That was the good news. All of the out of town guests were still planning on being there.

But...

Someone had started the local rumor mill going. And it turned out that almost every local guest who wasn't family or a very close family friend had thought the wedding was cancelled. Some were still willing to come—it was the wedding of Mason Maxwell after all and his family was very important in the valley—but others had made other plans and weren't willing to cancel them.

When I tried to point out that this was a wedding and

their other plans were likely far less of a life milestone than that, more than one told me they were going to a different wedding that night. The wedding of someone named Margaret Kepper who was going to have a six-foot ice sculpture and ride into the ceremony on live horses. A wedding it turned out these people had originally planned on attending until Jamie's wedding was announced when they'd changed their minds because Jamie's sounded fancier.

(It seems that was before the addition of the ice sculpture and live horses.)

Sigh.

By noon the two-hundred-person guest list was down to one-twenty-five. Looking on the bright side, it made finding a caterer and venue easier at least...

Or so my optimistic, turn-lemons-into-lemonade side had decided. But my pessimistic, this-is-only-going-to-get-worse side was wondering what next. Locusts? Balls of fire falling from the sky?

If Jamie hadn't been through that disaster with Ted Little and if she wasn't already planning to spend the entire month of January in Paris for her honeymoon (not the best of months to be in Paris, by the way, but, it was still Paris) I would've probably just called her up and urged her to move the wedding. To spring, maybe? (Give it a full year before she committed her life to Mr. Stone and Wood Everywhere.)

But she needed this win.

So I spent the next three hours calling every caterer I could find in a four-hundred-mile radius.

Unfortunately, all of the good ones were already booked up because: New Year's Eve. Which left me with one of two choices: hire someone who'd probably give all the guests food poisoning or really awful-tasting food, which for someone like Jamie who knew how to cook would be devastating and ruin the day, or...

Swallow my pride and reach out to the one person I knew could probably step up and make this happen, Jean-Philippe Gaston, invited wedding guest, acclaimed French chef, and my freshman year mistake.

(Technically, he was also Jamie's freshman year mistake. Although she didn't consider him a mistake. More a fun diversion. When he moved on to *her* roommate she just laughed it off and moved on to his roommate to make things convenient. Me, I spent the rest of the semester brooding about how he'd suckered me into thinking I actually meant something to him and second-guessing the motives of every single guy who tried to hit on me.)

Not someone I wanted to talk to or ever see again. But he was already coming to the wedding. And he did know how to cook if that Michelin star meant anything. So he really was the ideal solution.

But...Ugh.

Rather than do what I knew I needed to do, I took Fancy for a walk instead, relishing the feel of ice-cold wind blowing against my cheeks as we shoved our way through the six inches of snow that had fallen overnight.

Sometimes if I give my mind time, I come up with better ideas. But at the end of a blisteringly cold thirty-minute walk that had Fancy practically bouncing with joy and me so frozen I made a cup of peppermint tea instead of reaching for my usual Coke, the conclusion was the same: I needed to call Jean-Philippe and ask for his help.

I sighed and sank into the kitchen chair, staring at my phone. Best to just get it over with. Like pulling off a Band-Aid, right?

He owed me. And her.

CHAPTER ELEVEN

WITH EACH RING OF THE PHONE I DESPERATELY WANTED to hang up, but I didn't.

"Oui?" He answered with that sexy accent and deep voice that had so mesmerized me when I was eighteen.

"Jean-Philippe. It's Maggie Carver. Remember me?"

"But of course, Maggie. How are you? I am looking forward to seeing you at the wedding. You are still single, yes?"

(I might have also repeated the mistake of falling for his charms at my friend Julie's wedding as well as my friend Kate's wedding, but let's not go there.)

"No, actually. I will be there with my boyfriend." And, man, did that feel good to say.

"Ah, this is so sad. Have you just called me to break my heart?"

"No. Actually, I need a favor. A very big favor."

"Ah, yes? And what favor can I do for you, Maggie, who is no longer single?" he purred.

I rolled my eyes. Some people never change. "I need you to do the catering for Jamie's wedding."

He laughed but when I didn't say anything else, he stopped. "Mon Dieu. You are serious? You want me to cater a dinner in some itty bitty town in Colorado with no notice? Maggie…"

Time to turn on the charm. "It's only a hundred and twenty five guests, Jean-Philippe. And I know if anyone can do it, you can. Actually, you may be the only one who can save this wedding. Jean-Philippe, please…"

He chuckled. "Ah, you always knew how to get to my heart, Maggie."

I snorted.

"It is true. You are special to me."

"Just not special enough for you to keep your attention focused on just me, yeah?"

(I know, I was trying to convince him to do me a favor, so I shouldn't have pointed out his flaws, but I am what I am and that includes someone who is not always guarded with their opinions.)

"The world is full of beauty, Maggie. Am I to deny that beauty for the love of one woman?"

"That's pretty much how it's supposed to work, yeah."

"Pah. That is so provincial. My love for you is pure, Maggie. The rest…It is something else, yes? It is a celebration of life. Of the beauty of a woman. Of the way two people…"

"Oh, seriously. Stop. Just stop." I took a deep breath. "Will you do this? Please. Jamie needs you."

His accent mellowed as he turned serious. "This is not a simple thing. And I will not use some other man's menu. It must be my own creation. I am an artiste not a copycat."

"Of course. Understood. At this point I'm just trying to avoid feeding Jamie's guests mac 'n' cheese for dinner. Let me know what you need and we'll get it for you, okay? But there are some guests with food allergies and diet preferences, so if you can account for those as well..."

"Diet preferences? What is this?"

"Some people don't like red meat. Or dairy. Or carbs. Or sugar. Or any of those things."

"You want me to feed these people cardboard? I cannot use cream? Or potatoes? Or beef? Or bread?"

"It's just a few people. Please. No one is asking you to make them cardboard. But if you could have a couple options that take into account those dietary preferences, it would be very much appreciated."

He huffed. "I will try. But you tie my hands. I cannot be the genius I am when my hands are tied."

"Understood." I rubbed my forehead to keep from saying anything damaging. "Just, please do the best you can. And, Jean-Philippe?"

"Yes?"

"Do not let anyone else tell you this is cancelled or that there are any changes. I am the only one you should listen to. And only if I call you. Do not take orders from me via email."

"What is going on here, Maggie? What are you not telling me?"

I briefly told him about the person who was trying very hard to cancel Jamie's wedding.

"Why did you not tell me about this at first? I would have immediately said yes. And who would do this to Jamie? She is the sweetest."

"I don't know. But I'm going to find out. Until then... Talk to me and only me. Got it?"

"Yes, of course. We will make this work. You and me, Maggie," he made a kissing noise, "we are good together..."

43

"Haha. No. No, we are not. See you soon, Jean-Philippe."

I hung up the phone wondering what I had ever seen in that man. All I can say is I guess we all have that phase where a sexy foreign accent and intense interest can override common sense. But at least he'd help. That meant a lot.

Next step, figuring out *where* to host the wedding. Like that was going to be easy.

CHAPTER TWELVE

BEFORE I COULD START MAKING CALLS TO FIND somewhere to host the wedding, my grandpa came home. He's normally a reserved sort of man, calm like a good country lake. You know there's depth there and things you're not seeing, but it seldom ruffles the surface. So to see him agitated like he was made me immediately set aside everything and focus on him.

"Hey, Grandpa. What's wrong?"

"Lesley's grandkids are going to be staying with her for the rest of the week. Last-minute request by her daughter." He sat down across from me at the dining room table which was now my war room, all five of Jamie's binders spread across its surface along with all of my notes and ideas.

He didn't even look close to his eighty-two years of age. More like sixty, probably because his hair was still a light brown and he was trim and active in a way most men his age weren't anymore. I was glad to see he'd switched back to his standard flannel shirt, this one long-sleeved in honor of the season, and jeans.

It was good to have him around. To have something in

life that felt like it would always be there even though that's absolutely not the way life actually works.

I tilted my head to the side and studied him. "Do you think this was some move by Lesley's daughter to keep the two of you apart? I mean, kinda pointless now, isn't it?"

He shrugged one shoulder. "Could be. She doesn't know we're married yet."

"Why not?"

"Lesley wanted to wait a bit. At least until the new year. You know how some of her family doesn't exactly approve of me."

Sort of understandable given the fact that he'd shot her sister's husband when the man tried to kill her, a set of facts that not everyone in the family agreed upon. At least some didn't agree about how that man, who'd shown up with a gun and threatened everyone in the room, deserved to die. (That was the first time my grandpa went to prison.)

"Well, not like it's going to get any better unless you find a way to bring them around to your side. You could stay with Lesley and help take care of the kids…"

He snorted. "No. Those kids are spoiled brats. Last thing I need is to alienate Lesley's daughter by putting one of them in their place." He glanced around the house. "Maybe I'll clean up here a bit instead."

I hunched my shoulders as I followed his gaze. It wasn't *dirty*. There weren't weird smells or anything. But it was certainly much more cluttered than my grandpa normally allowed. What can I say? If a surface is free it seems like the perfect place to set a coat, the mail, or whatever else happens to be in my hand when I feel like setting it down.

"No, don't do that. I should do it. It's my mess. Why don't you work on one of your miniatures?"

My grandpa loved to assemble miniature planes. He was

very good at it even though it took him a lot longer than it had in the past. But he still had the patience for it. He'd sit there for minutes working to place just one little piece when his hand started shaking.

"Nah. I'm too wound up for that. It's okay. I need something to do. I'll just dump whatever's yours on your floor and then you can deal with it from there."

I grimaced, wondering if I'd have any space left on the floor when he was done. At least the steps I'd built for Fancy were free to use. After the first couple weeks she'd decided she didn't like them and never set foot on them again.

"Just don't move anything from this table, okay?"

"Where are we supposed to have dinner?"

"In the kitchen. Or on the couch. I mean, Lesley's family now, right? And Matt is…Matt. We don't really need to eat at the dining room table anymore, do we?"

"Maggie May. Unless you are married to that man we are not going to have him over for dinner and make him eat it on the couch or in the kitchen. That is not acceptable. Your grandma's probably rolling over in her grave right now at the mere suggestion of having a guest sit on the couch for dinner."

I wanted to object, but his house, his rules. So I just nodded instead. "Yes, sir. If Matt comes over for dinner, I promise I'll clear the dining room table."

"How's it coming along? You find replacements for everyone yet?"

"No. Not yet. I've only taken care of the caterer so far."

"You found someone?"

I nodded. "Jean-Philippe Gaston. Thanks to our saboteur Jamie's wedding is now being catered by a Michelin-starred chef."

"Isn't he that French fool who messed up your head when you were in college?"

I shrugged. "He may be a lot of things, but he's also a good cook who was already coming to the wedding. And most important, he was willing to help."

"Hm." My grandpa was not a fan of Jean-Philippe. He'd heard just enough over the years to probably want to have a private chat with him about how you treat a man's grand-daughter. A chat I would love to witness but also hoped never happened. "I look forward to meeting him."

"Just promise me you'll wait until after the food is served to put him in his place?"

He chuckled, finally relaxing. "Promise. Anything I can do to help?"

"Do you know someone who can get their hands on enough baby pink roses for a wedding in less than ten days?"

"Hm. No, not the roses. But I might be able to put something else together. Especially if you're okay with a Christmas theme."

"At this point? I'll take anything. Now to find a venue..."

I reached for my phone, hoping I'd have better luck with finding a venue than I'd had with finding a caterer.

CHAPTER THIRTEEN

I DIDN'T. EVERY MEETING HALL, CONFERENCE SPACE, ballroom, and barn in the entire valley was booked up for the holiday. Why Jamie had decided to get married on New Year's Eve, I did not know. I was pretty much ready to pull my hair out by the time Matt came by for dinner.

Like the dutiful granddaughter I am (or at least pretend to be) I cleared off the dining room table and set it with the nice china. Why I had to do so when it was just Matt coming over, I did not know. But my grandpa's house, my grandpa's rules.

I realized as I did so that I still hadn't even started on figuring out who was responsible for the mess I found myself in.

After I'd served up fifteen-minute chicken chili and my grandpa had cut up chunks of corn bread I asked, "Either of you know Mason Maxwell's former fiancée, Elaine something or other?"

"Oh, so you've heard about Elaine?" my grandpa asked.

"You knew about her then? And you didn't tell me?"

"Maggie May. What was the point? Mason had moved

on and was clearly madly in love with Jamie. And I know you. You'd want to tell Jamie, and I saw no point in that."

"Well, then. Tell me about her. Do you think she's the type to sabotage his wedding in revenge?"

"Elaine?" My grandpa shook his head.

"Definitely not." Matt slipped Fancy a bit of cornbread before taking a bite of the chili and making a pleased little hum in the back of his throat.

"Why not? What's she like?"

Matt and my grandpa exchanged a look before Matt answered. "Forgettable? Quiet? Mousy?"

"Hey sometimes the quiet ones are the crazy ones."

"Not really. That's usually only on television shows or in books to keep it interesting. In my experience, and I am a cop, most people who do something like that, there were signs beforehand. A little flash of temper, a fight here or there, or they just made people feel uncomfortable for no good reason. But Elaine? Nah."

"What does she do?"

"She's a bookkeeper. Works for the Mason family trust."

"So he still sees her on a regular basis?" I asked, outraged.

"Oh calm down, Maggie May." My grandpa shook his head. "Some people can date and move on like it was nothing."

"They were engaged!"

"Eh. Small town. Not a lot of choices, especially if you wait too long. She was nice enough, pretty enough, and his family liked her. So he asked her to marry him. But there was no spark."

What a horrible description of a future marriage. Nice enough? Pretty enough? Ouch. Let me never have an "enough" marriage.

"Well, the same about not having a lot of choices must go for her, too, right?" I asked. "Mason Maxwell, and I hate that I'm saying this, is quite a catch. She must've felt resentful when she lost him."

Matt shook his head. "Pretty sure she's just not capable of that kind of emotion, Maggie."

"Yeah, well, I'll see for myself. Where can I find her tomorrow?" Both Matt and my grandpa gave me disapproving looks, but I ignored them. "Well?"

My grandpa answered, "She should be at the Y. She's in charge of the charity clothes drive."

"Thank you. I'll swing by with Jamie on our way to Greta's."

"Greta's? Why are you going there?" Matt asked, slipping Fancy a bit of shredded cheese.

(I have to admit my heart swelled every time he gave her a bit of food from the table because it meant he loved my dog as much as I did. Even if it probably wasn't the healthiest choice for her. I was pretty sure I wasn't the only one who'd put on a few pounds since the barkery closed.)

I gave Fancy a rub on the top of her head as she looked to me for even more food, a thin line of drool coating her chest. "To fix the dress issue, hopefully. We'll see if Jamie is as willing to think outside the box as I am when it comes to weddings."

Matt raised an eyebrow. "How so?"

"Well, Greta has an insane number of gorgeous gowns in her closet. She had them shipped here after she decided to stay. But I doubt most of them are white. Which means if Jamie is willing, we can find her an absolutely beautiful gown to wear on her wedding day, but it may not be a traditional color."

"That's probably not going to work. Doesn't every bride want to wear white?"

"Not me. White gets dirty. I would not want to spend what's supposed to be one of the biggest days of my life worrying about whether or not I sat in something. And I certainly don't want to eat food in a white dress." (Not to mention sweat stains.) "Honestly. Why would I wear a color I haven't worn since I was a teenager just because it's tradition?"

"So you're thinking about marriage, are you? About being a bride?" Matt grinned.

I choked down my last bite of chili. "Only because I'm planning this for Jamie. And let me assure you that the more planning I do, the more I realize that a wedding is absolutely not what I want."

He leaned back, arms crossed as my grandpa glared daggers at me. "How so?"

"Well, take the expense, right? For *one* day. I'd rather use that money to go visit my friends and let them meet my husband that way than have them all fly in for a day where I'm so stressed and busy I barely have a chance to speak to them. Plus...I mean, I lost both my parents. There is no way I could have a wedding and not be reminded of that fact. Sure, my grandpa could probably walk me down the aisle, but I'd be thinking about how my dad wasn't there to do it the whole time and I'd be aware every single step down that aisle that my mom wasn't in the front row crying happy tears. Who wants to be that sad on one of the happiest days of their life?"

"Okay, making sense so far. What else?"

I didn't trust the mischievous gleam in his eye, but I figured I better get it all out while he was willing to listen.

"Well, we already talked about the white dress thing. So

not me. Give me a brilliant blue any day of the week. And wedding rings? Again, why? Do I really want to spend the rest of my life with this gigantic rock on my hand that will snag on everything? I have no objection to making a commitment to someone and wearing a symbol of that commitment for the world to see, but I'd far rather it was a simple band than what every other girl seems to want."

"A commitment to *someone*, huh?" Matt asked. "No one in particular?"

I rolled my eyes. "Matthew Allen Barnes, do not even get me started. I love you. I have told you that. Right now, in this moment, if there were anyone who was that someone it would be you. But I am a woman of many, many layers and you have barely scratched the surface so don't go getting all forever on me when you don't know what you're getting yourself into."

He grinned. "You're not supposed to know everything about someone when you marry them, Maggie. That's what the rest of your lives are for."

"Ha. You are so like a girl." I stood up from the table even though I probably would've had another serving if Matt hadn't thrown me so bad. "If you'll excuse me, I have to go make a list of people who might want to sabotage my friend's wedding. You two...I don't know. Bond or whatever."

My grandpa shrugged and looked at Matt. "What do you say to a game of Scrabble?"

"Sounds good. I'll get the board." Matt squeezed my shoulder as he walked past me. Part of me wanted to shrug him off but an equally big part of me wanted to bury my head against his chest and just let him hold me for a while.

This relationship business was not easy.

CHAPTER FOURTEEN

WHILE MATT AND MY GRANDPA ENGAGED IN A FIERCE game of Scrabble that I was surprised didn't draw blood, I tried to brainstorm who might want to ruin Jamie's wedding.

I had Elaine from Mason's side of things, but I figured it was much more likely that one of Jamie's exes had decided to get a little payback.

Jamie's a great person. And she loves everyone. It's one of her more endearing traits. But, well, let's just say that when it comes to affairs of the heart she's not always the most thoughtful. (Refer back to the fact that she loves everyone.)

Unfortunately for her there are men out there who just like me nurse their wounds after a relationship ends, no matter how casual. And Jamie, well, she's never really realized that.

So I wasn't surprised that she'd invited Ed to the wedding. A love interest from high school who chose to go to CU because Jamie was going there even though he had a full-ride scholarship to MIT. Also the guy she broke up with on Valentine's Day their freshman year so she could spend the rest of the day with a guy she'd met two weeks before and fallen head over heels for.

He went on my list for sure.

Then there was Brad. The first guy who'd ever asked her to marry him. She broke his heart when she said no even though how he could've thought she'd say yes I don't know. He followed her around like a lost puppy dog for the next three months until she finally set him up with one of her co-workers. They'd dated for two years until that woman also turned down his proposal.

So he went on the list.

So did Caroline, one of Jamie's friends from high school and sorority sisters in college who was the very definition of frenemies. At first glance you'd think they'd make perfect friends. They looked a lot alike, had the same interests, had the same taste in men. But that was exactly the problem. Every time Caroline took an interest in some guy, Jamie would accidentally steal him away.

(And I promise you, it was never intentional. Jamie would just shrug and move on if anyone ever told her they were interested in some guy, because plenty of fish in the sea and all. But just because Jamie moved on, didn't mean the guys turned their attention back to Caroline. It was ugly.)

And, of course, if they both joined a club Jamie ended up President and Caroline ended up Secretary. That was just the way it was. And since Caroline had announced her engagement a month before Jamie's and Jamie's wedding was now going to occur six months before Caroline's, she definitely had to go on the list.

As did Bethany who was trashy enough to ruin someone's wedding just because, why not, sounds like fun, especially if it involved poking at someone as put together as Jamie.

(Why Jamie stays friends with certain people, I will never know. Me, I'd kick them to the curb. But Jamie just shrugs it off. I guess I should be grateful for it, since she's also stayed friends with me all these years despite my sharp edges.)

I also had to consider the local angle. Who else was local that would want to see Jamie and Mason's wedding ruined? Because someone had started those rumors. And only a local could've pulled that one off.

I put Katie Cross's mom, Georgia, on the list for good measure. There'd never been love lost there and after everything that happened with Katie…Well.

I debated putting Lucas Dean on the list, but what was the point. He wasn't the type to do something like that and I didn't have time to bother with him. Knowing my luck, he'd demand an apology and he wasn't going to get it.

(One of his oh-so-accommodating defenders—i.e., a middle-aged woman he flirts with like the rabid dog he is—had the audacity to pull me aside the last time I was at the library and hand me a copy of Colorado's age of consent statute, because she didn't think it was fair that I kept calling what he'd done with Katie illegal when it was perfectly acceptable under Colorado law. I informed her that, thankfully I had never personally had to look up that law seeing as I wasn't trying to sleep with high schoolers, but thanks for the info. I also added that just because the law said a man of any age could legally sleep with a seventeen-year-old *girl* didn't make the whole thing any less skeevy and disgusting in my opinion. She walked away in a huff and hasn't spoken to me since. I consider that a good thing.)

Anyway.

I can't believe Jamie invited Lucas Dean to the wedding. But I didn't think he was behind this. So I put it aside.

That gave me six people to start with, which was plenty. I figured I'd run the list by Jamie the next day and see what she had to say about them.

(I wasn't planning on telling her about the sabotage, but I could ask, "Why did you invite that person?" without rousing any suspicions. Or so I hoped.)

CHAPTER FIFTEEN

THE NEXT DAY DAWNED COLD AND CRISP. BEING IN THE Colorado mountains in wintertime is wonderful if you're there to ski, which I don't. Or if you can stay inside the whole day, because then you get all that snowy beauty without having to deal with the cold. But between Fancy wanting to go for yet another freezing-cold walk and then having to pick up Jamie and drive to Greta's, that wasn't an option.

It was still beautiful. That snow-capped mountains' majesty is not just some lyric in a song. And the roads were actually clear enough to drive on without danger. But cold and I do not go well together. At least I was lucky enough to have some extra padding here or there from my lifestyle choices so I wasn't completely freezing.

(How do skinny women do it? I used to work with a woman who was always cold even in the middle of summer. Body fat has its uses, you know.)

Jamie, at least, was looking much better. She was back to her put-together self, her hair pulled back into a jaunty ponytail and wearing subtle makeup that gave her a bit of a cat eye. Her bright pink snow coat topped it all off with cheer.

For that alone, I was glad I'd taken on the role of wedding planner.

As we drove the twenty minutes towards Greta's, Jamie babbled on and on about the party favors and the cupcakes she was going to make. She'd decided to forego the traditional wedding cake in favor of five flavors of cupcakes formed to look like a wedding cake and had been experimenting with flavors the last few days.

Her final list included carrot cake, vanilla cream, and chocolate peppermint for the traditionalists. And then lavender pumpkin and basil strawberry balsamic for the more adventurous.

She'd tried a bunch of much crazier flavors than that— including a habanero chocolate caramel pecan—but decided that maybe her wedding wasn't the time to roll them out to a mass audience, so she was saving those for the café at the new pet resort instead.

"Thank you so much for this, Maggie," she said as we drove into Bakerstown. "I would've never thought of asking Greta if she had something that would work for the wedding. I mean, the dress I ordered was so perfect, but…"

"Right. No way you can gain fifty pounds in a week. Although, worst case scenario, we could stuff the dress until it fits you…"

She laughed. I was glad to see she was feeling better about the whole situation. I was pretty sure a few days ago she would've burst into tears at my joke instead.

"Hey, do you mind if we swing by the Y?" I asked. "I have some old clothes I want to drop off for the clothing drive."

(I'd already told Greta we were going to be delayed while I checked out Elaine.)

"Sure. No problem. I wish you'd told me. I could've brought some of my own."

"Like that hideous outfit you had on the other day? I mean, not that I can judge since I pretty much wear jeans and plain t-shirts anymore, but it was definitely not you. Where did you even get it?"

"My mom sent over all my old clothes from high school. And I was so bummed that morning I just wanted something familiar and comfortable to wear."

"That's what you used to wear in high school? Weren't you a cheerleader?" (Jamie and I hadn't become good friends until college.)

"I was. But I did wear clothes like that sometimes. Mostly on the weekends when I was helping my dad out around the cabin."

"Ah, that makes sense." I pulled into the parking lot for the YMCA. It was more crowded than I'd expected and I wondered how I was going to manage to find this Elaine woman and confront her long enough to determine if she was the saboteur.

(I think I'd been watching too many episodes of *The Mentalist* lately. That's the problem with binge watching shows, they stick in your head until you start to think like the main characters. So I was all Patrick Jane as I walked through the door, ready with a witty, "Are you the killer?" type question and a keen eye for deception.)

Fortunately for my diabolical plan, Elaine was the one in charge of the clothing drive, so the lady at the front desk sent us right to her.

"Are you Elaine?" I asked as Jamie and I walked up to a

long folding table at the back of the gym with two large bags of clothes in our arms.

"I am."

I tried not to stare. *This* was the woman Mason Maxwell had been engaged to before Jamie? She really was mousy. I mean, nothing wrong with being that way, but it was hard to believe that a man who'd been drawn to my friend's bubbly effervescence had at one point proposed to this quiet and reserved woman.

She had dishwater brown hair, pulled into a bun at the nape of her neck, and small mud-colored eyes. She was wearing makeup, but not well. At least her clothes were nice enough.

"I'm Maggie Carver. I don't think we've met." I held out my hand.

"No, we haven't."

Her hand hung limp in mine when I shook it. (I hate weak handshakes. I don't know why. They make me want to wipe my hand off on my pants afterward like maybe that lack of strength will somehow transfer to me like a bad virus.)

"And this is my friend, Jamie Green. Have you two met?"

They both shook their heads. "But I've heard good things about you," Jamie beamed at Elaine. "Elaine works for Mason's aunt at the family trust office. She says you're highly competent."

Elaine nodded, but didn't make eye contact. I couldn't rule her out as our mystery saboteur. I needed to get to know her better.

I glanced at the waist-high bins behind the table. "So do you take the donations and then sort them into those bins?"

Elaine nodded and waved towards a huge pile of

unsorted clothes and bags off to the left. "I have to get through all of that today. It's the last day for the drive and they're going to pick everything up at five."

"Well, let us help you then. If that's okay?" I looked back and forth between Elaine and Jamie who both nodded.

"Great." I took off my jacket and gloves and hid them away where they wouldn't get accidentally added into the donation bins. "Let's do this."

CHAPTER SIXTEEN

An hour later I was convinced that Elaine was exactly what she appeared to be—a kind but unassuming woman who really did not have it in her to hurt anyone for any reason. Either that or she was the most cunning psychopath to walk the earth. Because her persona did not change for that entire time.

Jamie being Jamie she managed to draw Elaine out probably as much as it was possible to do. They talked about high school and growing up in the area and going tubing and being a member of the local girl's adventure group as kids and how absurd that had been. (Elaine was a bit younger, so they hadn't been in the group at the same time, but the pack leader or whatever she was had been the same and it sounded like she was quite the character.)

By the end of the hour Jamie had invited Elaine to the wedding. I opened my mouth to suggest that wasn't the best idea, but Elaine beat me to it with a demure comment about how she really didn't like big social events.

"Oh, I'm right there with you," I said. "If it wasn't my

best friend getting married I'd be at home on New Year's Eve snuggled up with a book and my dog."

That was the one time I saw Elaine smile. It was a bright flash that transformed her face for just a moment and I realized that maybe under that quiet surface was a woman Mason Maxwell could've fallen for.

"That's where I'd like to be," she offered.

We then, of course, had to show each other photos of our respective dogs. She had a cute mutt that was part Australian Shepherd named Zela.

"I'll envy you on New Year's," I said, putting away my phone.

"Oh, I'm actually going to be at Margaret Kepper's wedding. We grew up together. I'm one of her best friends." She blushed as I tried to reconcile this quiet woman being friends with a woman who it seemed was anything but quiet.

"I heard it was going to be quite the event," I said.

Jamie paused in winding a bright turquoise and yellow scarf around her neck. "I didn't know Margaret Kepper was getting married that night, too."

"Oh, yes. It's been all anyone could talk about for months. It's going to be at her father's estate, which is absolutely amazing. They're even bringing in some fancy chef from New York to cater the whole deal."

I pursed my lips. "So she's not using anyone local? Like the Baker Valley Catering Company?"

"Oh no. She wanted better than that."

Well then she hadn't been the one to take Jamie's caterer away.

I nodded. "Someone told me her wedding dress is from some exclusive couture house in Paris. Supposedly it took seven months to do all the hand beading on it."

"That's what they say." Elaine was back to not making eye contact.

I turned to Jamie. "Do you know her?"

"Not really. She was a few years behind me in high school. She, um…They used to call her Mousy Margaret."

Elaine nodded. "Yeah. They actually called us the Mouseketeers when we were in middle school. But that all stopped after Margaret got her braces off and spent the summer with her aunt in New York. She came back looking amazing." Elaine ran a hand over her frizzy hair. "From that point forward, she ruled the school. All the boys wanted her and all the girls wanted to be her."

Jamie laughed. "Well, good for her for turning things around."

"Yeah. It was…awesome."

"So you guys have kept in touch then?" I asked.

"Sort of. Um. Yeah. We'd lost touch but then, um…" She glanced at Jamie. "We started hanging out again the last couple years you know after, um…Anyway. I better let you guys get going if you're going to make your lunch."

On the spur of the moment I grabbed a business card from my wallet and scrawled my phone number on the back. "Hey, you ever want to take your dog for a walk or something, call me. I'd be happy to join you."

Elaine nodded and tucked the card away. "Okay. Thanks."

I knew she probably wouldn't call, but she struck me as the type of person who could use another friend or two. And I have a weak spot for social orphans. I'm always reaching out to that person hiding in the corner or against the wall. Probably because I am that person more times than not and I know a kindred soul when I meet one.

As we got back in the van I mentally crossed Elaine off my list of suspects. One down, five to go. But first, time to find a wedding dress for Jamie.

CHAPTER SEVENTEEN

As we drove up the winding road that led to Greta's mansion, I wondered who on earth thought it was a good idea to live on the top of a mountain in a snow-packed area like this one. Sure the views were great, but the drive had to be hellish a lot of the time when it wasn't downright impossible.

But then I realized that most of the houses we were passing were probably used as tourist rentals and what would be unpleasant and annoying after three months of fighting through it was probably considered part of the adventure for someone in from Florida for the week.

At least the roads were well-plowed so my van didn't slip or slide at all.

I drove slowly as Greta's place came into view. It was definitely stunning with the two wings of rooms branching off of a central entryway and the Italian-style fountain (that was of course not running at the moment) in the center of an arched driveway with pristine snow in every direction until it hit the tree line. (In the summer that snow was a beautifully manicured lawn.)

After I parked I took a moment to stare out over the valley and admire the literally breathtaking view. Mountains on either side, covered in snow and evergreens, and Bakerstown and the valley spreading out below us like a picturesque little village scene you'd see on a postcard. Truly a million-dollar view.

Greta had the door open by the time I turned around, Hans, her Irish Wolfhound, at her side as always. "Greta!" I called. "How are you?"

I missed seeing her since the barkery closed. She'd come in with Hans almost every single day. And even though we still met at least once a week to discuss the plans for the pet resort, it just wasn't the same.

She made for an interesting friend. She was an ex-thief who'd been married so many times she'd lost count and was now worth hundreds of millions of dollars as a result. You wouldn't know it from her demeanor, but if you looked closely at the black slacks, jewel-toned tops, pale blonde hair, smooth skin, and tasteful diamonds they all pretty much screamed money.

We said our hellos as she led us into the sprawling entryway. I shuddered, remembering the last time I'd been there —a memory I'd rather forget.

"Where's your help?" I asked as she led us into the massive living room with a twenty-foot tall live tree in the center, festooned with white and silver ornaments punctuated with flat little red wooden horses and snowflakes.

"I did not need them today. I have made us lunch. It will be good, just us girls, no?" she said with her German accent.

"Oh, absolutely." I slowly turned, taking in the amount of space. "Hey, Greta, just out of curiosity, how many people could you host for a party in this place?"

I already knew she had an amazing kitchen, which Jean-

Philippe might need to borrow to prep. But if we could also use her place for the reception, that would be perfect, seeing as I still hadn't found a new venue.

"Two hundred? Two hundred and fifty, perhaps?"

"Really? In here?" Jamie asked.

"Oh, no. There is a ballroom. You have not seen it. Come. I will show you."

She led us to a corner of the house I'd never seen and opened a pair of double doors. Sure enough. There was a full-sized ballroom attached to the house. And it was as stunning as the rest of the place, all warm wood tones, pale marble, gold, and crystal. Something like that could easily be tacky if overdone, but she'd struck just the right note with it. (As she did with everything.)

Jamie stared. "Wow. You know, Greta, if I'd known you had this I might've asked to have my wedding here instead of at the convention complex. That space is functional, but this is...Amazing."

Greta and I exchanged a look. She knew about the wedding fiasco. The whole thing, not just the dress.

"Then we will do so."

"What? But...I've already booked the convention complex, I can't cancel now."

"She does not know?" Greta asked me.

Jamie turned to stare at me. "Know what?"

"Um, no, not yet."

Jamie looked back and forth between us. "What's going on? What aren't you telling me?"

I put an arm around her shoulders. "Well, I have some good news for you and some bad news for you. But first, let's get some drinks and food in hand, shall we?" Anything to delay the inevitable moment when I ruined my friend's day.

Jamie gave me a sidelong look, but she didn't ask

anything else as Greta led us to her amazing kitchen that looked like it had come straight out of a design magazine. Nor did she ask any questions while Greta dished us up an incredible breakfast-style casserole with eggs and bread and cheese and sausage that looked positively sinful but at least was balanced out by a bowl of fresh-cut fruit.

For drinks we had Bellinis. Who can go wrong with a drink made of peach and sparkling white wine? (Although I was sorely tempted to ask for just the wine. Or even better, the hard stuff. Not that I drink the hard stuff hardly ever, but shooting back a shot of whiskey seemed like a good plan in that moment.)

Jamie, not knowing what we were up against yet, watched Greta fill each champagne flute with a bit of skepticism. "It's not even noon yet. We should probably skip the alcohol, Greta."

"Nonsense. This is a ladies' brunch and a ladies' brunch always must have a bit of alcohol. It is not enough to get you drunk. It is just a polite amount to go with the meal."

We tapped glasses and dug into the food which was decadently delicious. "Greta, we're going to need to get this recipe from you for the resort," I said, trying not to shovel it all in at once.

"Thank you. It is my mother's recipe. Now. We must tell Jamie, no?"

"Tell me what?"

I set down my fork and downed the rest of my Bellini. "Turns out, the dress wasn't the only problem with your wedding."

She set her fork down, too, a panicked look in her eyes. "What do you mean?"

I opened and closed my mouth a few times, trying to

find the best way to explain things. Greta beat me to it. "Someone is trying to ruin your wedding, my dear. They cancelled your caterer and your reservation at the conference center. They ruined your dress. And they spread a rumor that the wedding had been cancelled as well."

So matter of fact. I flinched.

"But good news," I added, "is that we have a venue now, thanks to Greta. And will hopefully have a dress by the time we leave here. Also, thanks to Greta. And I've arranged for a new chef to cook for the wedding, so that's covered. And my grandpa is going to do something for the flowers. And we still have the pastor and the church and all of the out of town guests. So we're fine. It's all handled."

She bit her lower lip and I could see her struggling to be calm. "*Something* for the flowers? You mean I'm not going to have the baby pink roses I wanted?"

I clenched my fists under the table. Best to be as honest as possible. "No. You're not. But you are going to have a wedding. And it is going to be beautiful. And that's what counts."

"I've been dreaming about my wedding since I was six-years-old…"

When Greta refilled my champagne glass with straight Prosecco I cast her a grateful look before downing it in one gulp. She moved over to the second fridge and came back with an ice-cold can of Coke in hand. For that I wanted to kiss her. Instead I just said, "Bless you," before cracking it open and taking a long sip.

I grabbed Jamie's wrist and gave it a small squeeze. "Your wedding is going to be amazing, Jamie. I promise you."

"Is it? I mean, your wedding day is supposed to be so

special and...Now I'm not going to have the dress or the flowers or the reception area or the food I wanted..."

"It *is* going to be special, Jamie. As a matter of fact, it's going to be even more special than you'd planned."

"How?"

"Well, you already said Greta's ballroom is even better than the reception space at the convention center, right?"

"Yeah. I guess."

"And do you know who's going to cook the food for your wedding now?"

She shook her head, tears in the corners of her eyes.

"Jean-Philippe."

"Jean-Philippe? How did you manage that? I mean he's invited, but I would've never asked..."

"Exactly. But I did. So instead of a local caterer who is a nice man and makes good food you will now have a world-renowned chef feeding your guests. Although, I can't promise he's going to honor all of those dietary preferences all your friends had. But there will be food. And it will be good." I took another sip of my Coke. "Jean-Philippe may be a lot of things, but he's a damned fine chef. And with Greta's kitchen here, he should be able to put together a masterpiece."

She nodded, coming around a bit but not there yet. "But the dress...And the flowers..."

"Trust us, Jamie. And remember what matters most about your wedding day. You and Mason. Promising to spend the rest of your lives together. As long as that happens and you are strong in your love for each other, everything else is just window dressing. We'll make it beautiful window dressing, but the only thing that actually matters is you and Mason exchanging vows. And, fortunately, no one cancelled the pastor, so that's still good."

She nodded one more time, the panicked look finally leaving her eyes.

"Any chance you know who might have wanted to do this to you?" I asked.

"No. No one. I don't have enemies. And neither does Mason."

I pulled out my list of suspects. "This is who I came up with. Based on that, anyone else who should be on here?"

She glanced through the list and laughed. "You think Ed would try to sabotage my wedding? Why? He loved me. And what is Elaine doing on here? I don't even know her."

"Uh, well. Mason does."

"Through the family trust, but why would she want to sabotage my wedding for that?"

I winced. I hadn't planned on telling her about Elaine. "Because Mason broke off his engagement with her the first time he saw you."

Now, me, in that moment I would've turned white hot furious at the fact that the man I loved had been engaged and not told me, and the wedding would've probably been called off. (Many, many reasons I am single. Many.)

But not Jamie. She smiled. "Really? He never told me that. Oh, how romantic. It really was love at first sight for both of us, wasn't it?"

She put the list on the table, all sappy and happy. "I don't care who's trying to ruin the wedding. Let them. Nothing can come between us. What we have is true love."

I nodded. Sure it was. And, of course, love conquers all, right? Even horrible people trying to ruin your wedding. You just smile and voila it all works itself out.

Yeah, no.

But let Jamie think that. She was the bride-to-be. Let her have her illusions. I would be the dark enforcer who tracked down this horrible, awful person and got them to back off of my friend's special day.

"Well then," I said, forcing a smile. "That's settled. Let's find you a dress, shall we?"

CHAPTER EIGHTEEN

You know how on some of those home shows a person has a well-organized walk-in closet where all their clothes are on display on hangers and their shoes are lined up like artwork? Yeah, well compared to Greta's walk-in *room* of clothes that was a paltry, pathetic attempt at glamour.

The room we found ourselves in had to be ten foot by twenty foot. And it was all gowns, evening shoes, and little bejeweled bags on display stands. I don't even know where she kept her normal clothes. Probably in another equally-sized room.

There was one of those round seat things in the center of the room that comfortably sat all three of us and could've probably sat five more. And a large three-way mirror in one corner and a dressing screen in another.

I immediately sat down while Jamie slowly moved around the circumference of the entire room, almost but not quite touching all of the shiny and beaded dresses that hung from satin-padded clothes hangers. For Jamie, this had to be heaven. I knew she desperately wanted to try everything on and immediately wondered if I'd starve before I was allowed to finally crawl my way to freedom.

Not that I don't like fashion or looking nice. And some really high-end clothes do feel absolutely exquisite on, like they're made from some perfect body-hugging material that will hide every flaw with finesse. (All for the measly cost of a house in some portions of the country.)

It's just that I have a very low girly tolerance. And then I'm done. And ready for my pajamas and a good book and a Coke.

I hunkered down for a long afternoon while Jamie sighed in pleasure. "Greta...I just want to spend a day in this room watching you try on all of these clothes. They are amazing."

"You are going to spend a day in this room, but *you* will be trying on the clothes, no?" She poured each of us a glass of champagne and plunged the bottle back into the waiting ice bucket. "Now. Are we set on the color white? Is that the only choice?"

Jamie looked around the room at the rainbow of colors and then turned back to us, her eyes pleading. "I really would like to wear white for my wedding. Or maybe ivory. If I have to. But I've always pictured a dress that was snow white and like a cloud..." She glanced towards the one visible ivory dress in the corner.

Greta nodded. "Of course. Do not despair. We have many choices. I hide the white dresses. They are not as pretty to look at, no?"

I shook my head as Greta went to the far wall and pressed a button which rotated one of the rows of dresses until the entire visible wall of dresses was just gowns in shades from the purest white to the most delicate ivory.

"Greta, do you just come sit in here some days and stare at all of your beautiful clothes?" I asked.

She laughed. "Some days. But I like to look at my art more."

I still hadn't seen the painting that had led her to marry her last husband. I suspected not many people had since the painting was quite probably the original that she wasn't supposed to have based on his will. (She'd claimed when he died that his copy had been a forgery, but I knew better. She'd just pawned off a forgery on the museum he'd left it to so she could keep the original and actually see it. I guess once a thief, always inclined to blur the line as needed.)

She pulled three dresses and hung them facing outward so that we could see their silhouettes. The first was a long graceful sheath of pure white. The second was a princess-style dress in a softer shade of white with gold laced throughout the bodice and poofy skirt. And the third one was a short lacy affair of lightest ivory. "We will start with these."

Jamie stared, her mouth hanging open in awe.

"Careful there, Jamie. You might drool on the carpet." I took another sip of champagne, glad to see things were coming together so well.

That broke Jamie out of her trance. She grabbed the first of the three dresses like a kid in a candy store and went to the dressing screen to try it on.

It took two hours for Jamie to try on each and every dress that had any chance of working for the wedding. I honestly think she knew which one she wanted from the beginning, but decided to have fun with it. And why not? How often do you get the chance to try on that many beautiful dresses?

I wanted to be annoyed, but it felt so good to see my friend happy and carefree for once that I just smiled and drank.

I would've probably been drunk by the end of it if I hadn't switched back to Coke halfway through.

Jamie finally settled on the princess-style dress with the gold laced through the bodice and skirt. It suited her. And, better yet, only required minimal alterations, which Greta herself had volunteered to do.

(I silently wondered whether she was qualified to do so, but when she pulled out her sewing kit and got to work pinning the hem it was clear she was an experienced seamstress on top of everything else.)

"Greta," I said as she made her final checks and adjustments, "I have to say I'm surprised you owned a dress like this. I can't see you in something so...poofy."

She laughed. "Ah, yes. I do not believe I ever wore this one. My sixth husband? Perhaps my seventh? I can never remember. Dominic. He bought it for me." She took a sip of her champagne as she walked around Jamie looking for any last-minute adjustments to make. "That is when I realized that we were not as well matched as I had first thought."

She shrugged slightly. "He was a magnificent man, but not for me. And I, clearly, was not for him. But now we have Jamie's dress for her wedding, so it all works out eventually, no?"

"So it does."

"Would you like to try anything on, Maggie?"

I laughed. "Jamie tried that with me at one point. It turns out that you women are a lot more slender than I am. But thank you for the offer."

"Wait. I have not always been slender. And I have a dress that I think is perfect for you. One moment." She pushed a button to rotate the dresses on one of the other walls where all the blue and green shaded dresses were and then pulled out a dress and turned to show it to me.

It was stunning. A gorgeous sapphire blue that had a fitted V-neck bodice with no sleeves and then a multi-layered skirt that flared out from the hips but not so much that it felt princessy.

"It's...Wow, Greta. *That* is definitely my kind of dress. But..."

"Try it on. You may be surprised."

"I don't know..." It was gorgeous, but if it fit Greta it would probably not even fit over my head. Maybe I could wear it on one thigh.

"Just try it. You will not show us if it does not fit."

"Okay." I gingerly took the dress and disappeared behind the dressing screen. I really wanted it to fit, but I wasn't holding my breath. I figured I'd step into it, just in case. As I pulled it up to my hips I clenched my teeth, waiting for that moment when it would stick and go no farther, but it slid right on up.

Turns out it fit. Perfectly. Like it was made for me. I almost ran to the three-way mirror, turning in half-circles so I could watch the way the skirt flared out from my hips.

Greta clapped her hands together in pleasure. "I knew this dress was for you. You must keep it."

"I can't, Greta. I have nowhere to wear it." I already had a bridesmaid's dress for Jamie's wedding and since I ran around barefoot in pajamas most days it would be absolutely wasted on me.

"You will find something."

"Then let me pay you for it."

"Nonsense. We are friends, no? And you see how many dresses I have. It no longer fits me. But it fits you. You will take it."

I wanted to. Desperately. "But…"

"This will be your something blue for your own wedding. We all know you are not a woman in white."

I laughed. "Nice thought. But I am not getting married anytime soon. Like, seriously, not for a good decade."

Greta chuckled. "Ah, Maggie. You are much too serious about this relationship and wedding thing. You marry a man, it doesn't work, life is not over. You move on."

"I am not going through that more than once. Honestly, love you Jamie, happy for you, think it's great you're having this big wedding, but my ideal wedding is on the side of a frickin' mountain with the man I love and no one else around. Just us exchanging our vows. And a dress like this? Does not belong in that picture."

Greta nodded. "My third wedding was like that. We were married in an Italian vineyard, just us and the officiant. But there is no reason you cannot wear a beautiful dress for this mountainside wedding is there?"

I shook my head and went to change out of the dress even though I really didn't want to. I handed it back to her. "I appreciate the offer, Greta. It is truly a beautiful dress. But I…I just can't."

The way she pursed her lips, I knew this battle wasn't over, but she didn't say anything else so I decided I'd call it a temporary victory and get out of there before it became a rout.

CHAPTER NINETEEN

FURTHER WEDDING PLANS OR INVESTIGATION HAD TO GO on hold at that point because it was Christmas Eve and pretty much no one was available anywhere for any sort of calls or planning. (One more strike against the good ol' New Year's Eve wedding idea.)

But that was okay.

We were in a pretty good place. We had the church and pastor, we had a place for the reception, we had a caterer, we had a wedding dress, and my grandpa was doing something for the "floral" decorations. We also had enough guests to make it work and Jamie seemed on top of the cupcakes and party favors.

I did swear both Jamie and Greta to secrecy about the new reception location, though. I was just paranoid enough about the whole thing that I didn't want anyone to know we'd found somewhere until the last possible moment.

I figured I'd see if I could find some of those chartered party buses to ferry everyone from the hotel up to Greta's so that (a) no one would try driving that windy road with alcohol in their system and (b) I wouldn't have to reveal the reception location to anyone other than Jean-Philippe, his crew, and the decorators until the actual reception.

Which reminded me I needed to sort the booze issue. That was easier at least. Since we were now using a private home for the reception I could send Matt or Jack to a liquor store with a list of what to buy.

I figured I might even send one of them down to Denver for that since there were a couple of very large liquor stores down there that would have everything we could possibly want. Tipsy's and Applewood were both good choices. Except for the local beer I wanted. That I'd get straight from the brewery.

But for the time being I had to put that all aside and prepare for the holiday.

We'd all agreed not to exchange gifts. Matt and I were too new to being a couple for me to handle the pressure of what to get him for Christmas. And Grandpa and Lesley had spent their money on their trip to Vegas. So Matt, Jack, Trish, and Sam were doing Christmas morning at the trailer so Sam could get his gifts, and then they were going to come to our house for a Christmas lunch. Jamie, Mason, Lesley, Greta, Evan, and Abe were also coming over.

Which meant I had to make sure the house was properly decorated and that there was a good spread of food for twelve people. Fortunately we'd ordered in a baked ham and were serving it cold with bread and cheese and other sandwich-like accompaniments, which meant all I had to do was prepare a veggie tray, onion dip, deviled eggs, and dessert.

Onion dip is easy enough. You just dump and stir.

But deviled eggs…

If they weren't a family tradition and didn't taste so darned good I'd probably never make them again. But there's something about that tangy yolky yumminess that goes perfectly with a good ham. So I boiled the eggs and peeled the eggs and cut the eggs and scooped the eggs and made up the stuffing and stuffed the eggs and finished it all off with a dash of paprika.

I'd made two dozen eggs' worth, which I hoped would be enough.

I like to experiment with at least one dish each holiday to keep things fresh, but deviled eggs you do not mess with. You do not put tuna in them. (Gag.) You do not put relish in them. You do not add pickles. Or lobster. Or any of the other insane, crazy things people try to put in there.

Deviled eggs are sacrosanct. You only use eggs, mustard, mayo (or Miracle Whip), and vinegar. And just enough paprika to make them look somewhat enticing. (I once used too much paprika. It was not a good thing.)

Since I couldn't experiment with the eggs, I chose to experiment with dessert instead.

And because my experiments sometimes misfire badly, I made three desserts instead of just one. All were dips of one sort or another made with variations on whipped cream, pudding, or cream cheese combined with flavors like eggnog, pumpkin, or peppermint chocolate.

I have to say…Not bad. Light and fluffy for the most part except for my failure when I tried to combine two different ways to do things and the peppermint chocolate one turned into sludge. But the eggnog one was tasty. As was the pumpkin one. Especially with ginger snaps.

They were certainly easy to make, which is always appreciated when trying to accommodate a wide range of guests for the first time ever.

I had planned on spending the end of Christmas Eve with Matt, curled up in front of a nice fire like the couple we were, but with my grandpa banished from Lesley's because of the invasion of the grandkids, that didn't happen. Instead Matt, my grandpa, and I stayed up late drinking hot cocoa with real marshmallows in it and playing Scrabble.

I was actually getting better at it. I could almost hold my own against those two. I had to be careful not to make up words, which is a bad habit of mine, or to use slang that wasn't going to be in the official Scrabble dictionary, but I'd adopted a hybrid style that combined my grandpa's love of playing multiple words at once with Matt's style of trying to play seven-letter words on triple-scores.

I still lost. But only by four points. Not bad. Not bad at all.

I have to say, it was a good night. A really good one.

And certainly better than the year before when I'd gone out for drinks to a bar with a friend of mine. There's a sad desperation to people who hang out at bars on Christmas Eve. (Not that that's wrong if you're one of those people. Heck, I was one of those people the year before, wasn't I? But that one experience did make me think that next time around I'd just stay at home alone and drink. Because being in public and drinking alone on Christmas Eve? It's just...yeah.)

Anyway. Good Christmas Eve. All prepared for Christmas Day.

CHAPTER TWENTY

I'D LIKE TO SAY I SLEPT IN ON CHRISTMAS DAY. BUT WHO am I kidding, I had Fancy. And Fancy thought being up at the crack of dawn—or before it at that time of year—was the best possible idea in the world.

Also, it had snowed overnight. A lot. There was a solid foot of fresh powder in the backyard.

Which meant I started the day bundled up to my eyeballs shoveling Fancy a path through the backyard. I even made her two spaces where she could lie down.

And then, because she would not stop crying at me, we went for a walk. You do not understand how hard it is to walk through a foot of snow until you do so with a large black dog dragging you along at a very fast clip.

I figured that was my work out for the week.

When I returned my grandpa was seated at the kitchen table with his crossword puzzle, a steaming cup of coffee in his hand. I grabbed a Coke and joined him.

"You want me to make breakfast?" I asked.

"Maybe later. I should get out there and shovel the driveway." He quirked one eyebrow at me.

"Oh. The driveway. Right. And the sidewalk leading up to the house that all the guests are going to need to use..." It hadn't even occurred to me to clear those. I was just thinking of Fancy when I shoveled the backyard. "I can do those after breakfast."

"Do you know how to run a snow blower?"

"No. But you could teach me. Or I can just do it by hand."

He shook his head. "I'll do it."

I would've argued further, but I knew there was no point. As old as he was and as much as I thought I was there to take care of him there were certain tasks that in his mind were "men's tasks". Mowing the lawn and shoveling the driveway were two of them.

"Okay, fine. But after breakfast."

"Deal."

I quickly shot a text to Matt asking if he thought he could make it over to clear the driveway and sidewalk before my grandpa and I were done with breakfast. He texted back that he was already on his way and almost there. I felt that weird glowy sappiness that comes with being in love. He was such a good man.

I took my time preparing fried potatoes and a breakfast frittata with goat cheese, spinach, bacon, and sun-dried tomatoes. My grandpa gave the meal a side-eye as I was putting it together because he's never been one for "fancy" ingredients like that, but I knew he'd like it. At least I wasn't trying to make hand-squeezed orange juice or something. I figured that was one part of the meal that was perfectly fine coming out of the carton, thank you very much.

Matt timed it perfectly. He finished plowing the driveway clear with his truck just as I pulled the frittata out of the oven. I went to the window and waved him inside as I set a third place at the kitchen table for him.

"Maggie," my grandpa growled as he finally looked out the window and saw what Matt had done. "I am perfectly capable of shoveling my own driveway."

I kissed him on the cheek. "I know you are, Grandpa. But Matt was already on his way over when I texted him. Let him help. Please?"

He grumbled, but when Matt came inside, he just shook his hand and thanked him. Matt gave the perfect answer. "I knew you could clear it yourself, Mr. Carver, but I wanted to try that new slow plow I got and your driveway is perfect for it. Plus, I needed to get out of that trailer. Sam has been up since five playing with some new truck Jack got him that has lots of bright lights and makes really loud noises."

"He isn't going to bring that here, is he?"

"No, sir. I will make sure of it."

"Okay then. Let's eat this thing Maggie made for us." He hesitated about sitting at the kitchen table with company, but I just ignored him and sat down. It wasn't dinner. It was breakfast.

"It's good to expand your horizons every once in a while, Grandpa," I said as I served us each up a portion of the frittata.

"So you say." He poked at the food on his plate with a frown, but he stopped grumbling after the first bite, like I knew he would.

CHAPTER TWENTY-ONE

AFTER BREAKFAST I DRAGGED OUT THE TRIO OF PACKAGES I'd hid in my room.

"What's that?" my grandpa barked. "We said we weren't doing presents this year."

Matt nodded his agreement.

"And we're not. These are for Fancy."

"You bought your dog three Christmas presents? When she already has more toys than can fit in her toy bin and you make her so many different types of treats it's a miracle she doesn't have to be rolled through this house?"

Even my grandpa's orneriness wasn't going to get in the way of my enjoying the holiday and spoiling my dog. "Yes. Yes, I did."

I went to the back door where I could see Fancy lying in one of her little dug out spots in the yard, enjoying the morning. "Come on, Fancy," I called.

She looked at me and then looked away. There was a squirrel in a tree. Far more interesting than me and whatever I wanted her for.

"Fancy. Treat."

That got her attention. She slowly lumbered her way to her feet and followed me inside, but not all the way to the living room. She stopped in the kitchen and stared expectantly at the spot where I stored the salmon snaps.

I knew I could either try to push and drag her unsuccessfully into the living room or I could just give in and lure her there with a handful of treats, so I grabbed a handful and held it in front of her nose and then started walking towards the living room.

She followed along after me, leaving a trail of slobber in her wake.

"Maggie..."

"I'll wipe it up. Don't worry." I threw the treats in a pile on the carpet and reached for the first bag while Fancy ate up every last crumb and then started licking around to make sure she hadn't missed anything.

"Here, Fancy. Look." I handed her the toy first. It was a hedgehog with a Santa hat that made grunting noises. I made it grunt and she lunged for it, taking it delicately between her paws and starting to gum it to death.

She's not one of those dogs that destroys her toys. No torn pieces and stuffing everywhere. She's more like a stream relentlessly wearing away at a canyon wall. You have to keep an eye on things because what looks fine one moment will suddenly turn into a giant hole along a seam somewhere the next. But that's really why she has so many toys. Because I can usually sew those little holes back up and the toy will last another year, two, or more.

My grandpa crossed his arms as he watched her. "That seems like more than enough for her. What else did you get?"

I pulled out a collar with jingle bells on it.

"Maggie May..."

"What? It'll be fun. And she only has to wear it today."

"What a colossal waste of..."

"Grandpa. It's fun."

He grumbled at me. "In my day, dogs stayed outside. They didn't have beds. They didn't have toys. They didn't go to daycare."

"And they weren't good companions, were they? But Fancy is. She's the best. And you agree, I know you do. You may pretend not to like her, but you enjoy it just as much as I do when she curls up on the couch next to you at night to watch a little TV."

"I didn't say she can't be inside. But spending your hard-earned money on..."

"On a family member. Who always appreciates what I give her." I fastened the collar around Fancy's neck, but she was still absorbed in chewing on her new toy.

That stopped as soon as I opened the last bag. One of her favorite treats which I rarely gave her anymore since I made my own treats now. The toy was immediately forgotten as her eyes fixed on my hands. She sat at attention.

I gave her a kiss on the nose. "Good girl, Fancy. Here you go." She took the treat and ran out of the room, headed for the backyard. I just smiled. I loved that dog. More than anything.

Well, Matt was running a close second. And I loved my grandpa. But Fancy still took first place. And probably always would. It's easier with dogs. No real uncertainty or challenge. They just love so it's easy to love them back.

The rest of the day went well. It was great to have so many people I knew and liked gathered together to share food and company. I know the holidays have different meanings for different people, but for me that's always what Christmas and Thanksgiving have been about: friendship, family, and good food.

We were there for hours, eating, talking, and laughing. It was wonderful. And made me so glad to be where I was with the people I loved.

But the next day it was finally time to find my culprit.

CHAPTER TWENTY-TWO

I CALLED ED—MR. VALENTINE'S DAY BREAKUP—FIRST
since he was local and definitely had a reason to not want to
see Jamie live happily ever after.

He answered on the first ring. He sounded a bit like
Eeyore on the phone, all depression and slooow talking.
"Hello."

"Ed, it's Maggie Carver. How are you?" I added extra
cheer to my voice to counteract his mind-numbing effect.

"Hi Maggie. I'm fine. You?"

"Good. Good. So, are you excited about Jamie's
wedding? I saw you're coming."

"Jamie's wedding? Oh, yeah. When is that?"

"New Year's. You RSVP'd."

"Did I?" He thought for a long moment. A looong
moment. "Are you sure? It might've been my mom. She
thinks I should get out of the house more. Mooom!"

I heard his mother shout back in the background and
they proceeded to have a conversation about how, yes, his
mother had RSVP'd for him because there'd be a lot of

pretty single girls at a wedding and maybe he could meet one and move out of her house for once and all.

As soon as he got back on the phone, I made my excuses and hung up. Glad Jamie dodged that bullet. I would've had to stop being friends with her if she'd stayed with him because three minutes in that man's company and I wanted to start pinching myself to stay awake.

But he was off the list. Can't sabotage a wedding you don't even know about.

Brad, Mr. Failed Proposal, was next. That was a fast call. He was on his honeymoon in Hawaii with some cocktail waitress he'd met in Tahoe two weeks before. At least someone had said yes to him. I congratulated him and quickly got off the phone.

I was about to make my next call when the phone rang. It was the pastor.

"Pastor Nelson. How are you? How was your holiday?"

"It was delightful, Maggie, thank you. Although, this morning was not."

I sat up straighter, knowing whatever it was I did not want to hear it. "What happened?"

"I'm not exactly sure. It seems the furnace at the church stopped working sometime yesterday, although it looks perfectly fine. But the heat was off probably all day yesterday and until I arrived today."

I bit my lip, already knowing where this was going. "Is the church okay?"

"No. A pipe burst in the basement. The one that leads to the first-floor bathrooms."

When I didn't say anything he added. "You know how cold it got last night, Maggie. None of the bathrooms have running water."

I took a deep breath. I did know how cold it had gotten.

And I knew that whoever I was dealing with was the type of horrible, reprehensible person who'd damage a church to get their way.

What kind of person does that? I'm not the most religious of souls, but places of worship are supposed to be safe zones. People can be murdering one another in the streets, but never in a church. Or a mosque. Or a synagogue. Or what-have-you. You do not do that.

I glanced out my window at the sky wondering if I was going to see a bolt of lightning sometime soon. Because someone out there needed to be struck down.

"Pastor, I hate to say this, but I think you need to call Matt."

"Matt? Which Matt?"

"Matt Barnes. The police officer."

"Why?"

Bless his soul. The pastor didn't have the type of belief in other people that could see what must've happened. I had to be the one to burst that illusion. "Because I suspect that this was done by someone, it didn't just happen. Someone probably entered the church and turned off the heat after you left for the holiday."

"Why would someone do that?"

I filled him in on what had been happening with Jamie's wedding.

"But no one would do that to the church. Would they?"

"I'd like to say no, but well...Sadly I think that someone did."

There was a long moment of silence on the other end of the line.

"I'm sorry, Pastor. We'll find who did this. And Matt will punish them. I promise you."

"It's not punishment I'm after, Maggie. I believe in

turning the other cheek. But I've always felt like this was a good community. It's sad to see something like this happen. I can't think of a single parishioner who would do something like this. And there wasn't anyone at Christmas Eve service that I didn't recognize."

"I don't know what to tell you, Pastor. It only takes one bad apple. And sometimes they aren't that easy to see."

He sighed. "I don't know when we'll get this fixed, Maggie. Not before the wedding day, that's for sure. I don't even know how we're going to pay for the repairs to be honest. We're not a rich church. And neither is our congregation."

I thought about Mason Maxwell and his unlimited wedding budget. And Lucas Dean and the fact that he owed me whether he thought he did or not.

"It'll be fixed in time for the wedding, Pastor, don't you worry about that. And don't worry about the cost either."

"But how?"

"A combination of someone who is in love and has a seemingly bottomless bank account and someone who owes me enough that they'll do what I tell them to."

"Maggie, please don't intimidate anyone on our behalf."

I laughed. "Don't worry, Pastor. I won't." I was going to do it on Jamie's behalf. "Stay reachable, please. I'll try to have someone there today to fix it."

"Thank you, Maggie. God bless you."

"My pleasure, Pastor."

I hung up and called Mason.

"Mason Maxwell."

"Hey, Mason. Just so you know, your wedding bill now includes some plumbing work at the church. So when Lucas Dean bills you for it, please pay."

"What happened?" he snapped.

"Burst pipe. No working bathrooms. I suspect our saboteur is behind it."

"Who is doing this?"

"You haven't thought of anyone else?"

"No. I didn't even really think Elaine was capable of it. And Jamie said the list you came up with had no one on it she'd think was capable."

"Well, Jamie's a kind person. She doesn't see the bad in people."

"True enough. But this is...Personal. Trying to ruin a wedding. And who sabotages a church?"

"Exactly. That's a new level of low that most wouldn't stoop to. Well, you think of anyone, let me know. Right now, I have to go make an unpleasant call or two. Give Jamie my love."

"Will do."

I hung up and glared at the phone. I knew I needed to call Luke. He was the best contractor in the county and the only one I'd be able to browbeat into working between Boxing Day and New Year's. But...Ugh. The man was a slug. And I'd thought that before the Katie situation.

I walked to the fridge to grab another Coke, but realized it would be my fourth of the day which was extreme, even for me.

Instead I grabbed a beer. It was only one in the afternoon, but really, did it matter?

CHAPTER TWENTY-THREE

I'D JUST SAT DOWN AT MY COMMAND CENTER IN THE dining room when my grandpa walked through. "Maggie, what are you doing?"

"What? What's wrong?"

He glanced at his watch. "It's one o'clock in the afternoon."

"I know."

"You are still in your pajamas."

"They're comfortable." (I'd changed back into them after walking Fancy. No point in wearing my sweats, which were a little snug around the waist when I could wear my PJs instead.)

"And you're drinking a beer."

"I didn't want to have another Coke."

He glared at me, hands planted on his hips. "Have you heard of water?"

I shrugged a shoulder and took a sip of my beer. "I don't drink water."

"Or orange juice?"

"That's a breakfast drink."

"Kool-Aid?"

"That's as bad as having a Coke, sugar-wise. And don't you even suggest I have a glass of milk. It was Coke or beer. I chose beer."

He stepped closer. "I will repeat that it is one in the afternoon."

"Not like I'm going to have another one. I mean, if I'd had this beer with dinner you wouldn't even mention it. But because I have my one beer of the day before five o'clock it's somehow taboo? Or wrong? That's just silly."

"What are you going to have with dinner then?"

"I don't know. Maybe I'll have...water." I knew I wouldn't. Not that I was planning on having another beer. Probably another Coke, although that was less than ideal, too.

He crossed his arms. "Fine. You can have a beer at whatever time of day you want as long as it's the only one of the day."

"Yes, sir. Thank you, Dad."

He took another step closer. My grandpa is not a man you cross.

"Sorry," I said before he could light into me about my attitude. "I'm just a little stressed is all, trying to find whoever did this to Jamie. And now someone has sabotaged the church, too."

"That's no excuse, Maggie May, for living like a slob. You can have a beer, one beer, whenever you want to. But for crying out loud, put on some real clothes. No pajamas after breakfast."

I would've traded the afternoon beer for pajamas if there'd been a choice, but there clearly wasn't.

"Why?" I asked.

"It's a mindset thing, Maggie May. You wear pajamas all

day you turn into a sloth. You just sit around and do nothing."

I gestured to the table which was full of papers. "Does this look like nothing to you? I was just about to make a very important phone call."

"Well, put on real clothes before you do. My house, my rules."

I wanted to argue, but the fact was, it was his house. So it was his rules. But I did not enjoy the fact that I suddenly felt like a twelve-year-old kid again. I stomped off to my room to change, which meant I was not in a good mood when I finally called Lucas Dean.

"Ho, ho, ho, Merry Christmas, beautiful," he said as soon as he answered. "What? No FaceTime?"

"Shut up, Luke."

"Maggie, always such a sweetheart. You should come over. Share a cup of cheer. Although I hear you're off the market these days."

"I am. Not that I was ever on the market for you, Luke. I could see through your crap from day one, thank you very much."

"Ah, Maggie. Always such a stick in the mud. It'll be interesting to see if Matt can warm you up."

I started to count to five. I needed his help and lashing out at him for being a jerk wasn't going to get me what I wanted.

Before I hit four he asked, "Why are you calling?"

"I actually have a job for you."

"It's the holiday. I'm not working until the new year."

"This is for Jamie. You owe her, Luke."

"What do I owe her for?"

"For playing her all those years. For charming her while

messing around with anyone else you could get your hands on."

He chuckled. "Jamie never seemed to mind."

"Luke. You need to do this. For Jamie."

"If Jamie wants my help, I'm happy to give it. Tell her to call me."

"Look, Luke. I do not have time for this. I am offering you paid work. And you are going to take it."

"I am, am I?" I could see his cocky smile in my mind and wanted to smack it right off his face, but instead I forced myself to take a deep breath and step back.

"This *is* for Jamie, okay? And she's not calling you because I don't want her to know about it." I briefly told him what had happened so far and about what had happened at the church. "So, see, we need you. You are the only person I know who can pull off that kind of miracle in the time we have. And, good news, Mason's paying for it. So you get a little added bonus there. A client who will pay more than full price."

He didn't answer right away.

"Luke? Tell me you'll do this. Please?"

"Alright. For Jamie. But I'm charging double time and expenses."

"Fine."

"You have any idea who's doing this?"

"No. Must be someone local, though. I just don't know who it could be. Jamie isn't one to make enemies. People like her. And Mason, I can't see him doing anything extreme enough to make an enemy that would do this. You have any ideas?"

"I assume Georgia's already on your list? Scariest woman I've ever met."

"Yeah, she's there. And my next stop. Anyone else?"

"Can't think of anyone, but if I do...I'll call."

"Alright, thanks." I gave him the pastor's number and hung up.

Only then did I cringe, realizing I'd just thanked Lucas Dean of all people. And that I'd made him part of the reason Jamie's wedding was going to be a success. Ugh.

CHAPTER TWENTY-FOUR

I called Caroline—Ms. Frenemies—next since there was a chance she was already in the area for the holiday.

"Hey Caroline," I said with my fake friendly smile on as she answered her phone. "How are you?"

"I'm so great. I just got a major promotion at work and my Italian fiancé and I ran away to the Bahamas for the holiday to celebrate. We are currently beachside sipping Mai Tais." Arrogance just dripped off of her. Made me want to gag.

My only consolation was that her fiancé was probably half-bald and significantly overweight and the promotion she'd received was not as major as she'd want me to believe.

"So you aren't going to make it to Jamie's wedding then?" I asked.

"Right. That. Isn't it going to be in like a cabin or something?"

"No. Why would you think that?"

"Well, I mean that's about all there is in the valley, isn't it? It's not like it's Aspen or Vail. When I heard she'd quit her job to move *home*, I was just appalled."

"There's actually a very nice resort here."

"That's not a resort, that's a convention center."

"It has a very nice ballroom."

"Yeah. Right. So looking forward to it." The insincerity practically oozed through the phone. "Wouldn't miss it for the world. I mean she is one of my dearest friends, after all. Sisters forever, right? Maybe I can give a toast."

"Yeah, no."

"Why not? I'm one of her bridesmaids."

I made up a lie. "They're limiting toasts to close family. So sorry."

"Oh, well, whatever. What are you doing these days, Maggie? Are you going to hook up with Jean-Philippe, again? It's like a wedding tradition for you, isn't it?"

I took a deep breath and reminded myself that I was doing this for Jamie.

"Actually, Caroline, I have a boyfriend."

"Really? Who?"

"Matt Barnes."

"Isn't he a cop now? Ew. Dating down are you?"

If that woman had been there in person in that moment she may not have survived to the wedding.

"I don't think so. He's good to me. He's funny, he's intelligent. And he's damned good-looking."

(Sorry for the cussing, but I was annoyed.)

"Yeah, but he's a cop. Isn't that, like blue collar? I mean, why'd you get a college degree for that?"

I cleared my throat to prevent myself from saying all the things I wanted to say to her uppity little…self. "I didn't go to college to get my M-R-S degree, thanks. I've got that side of things handled on my own so I can just look for a good man who'll treat me right. Which is what Matt is. Look I gotta go. Buh-bye." I hung up.

That.... So many things I wanted to call her but I won't for politeness sake. I'm sure you can think of a few on your own.

How dare she judge Matt for, heaven forbid, choosing a career that helps people. A career that probably takes more interpersonal savvy and guts than ninety percent of people in this world even have. Not to mention the level of self-control and patience required.

What was her deal?

I was sure she hadn't sabotaged Jamie's wedding, but I decided to leave her on my list just for spite. Maybe if by the day of the wedding I hadn't yet found the culprit I could convince Jamie to let me ban her from the wedding just in case.

Or I could ask Matt to ask a friend to set a nice little speed trap for her. Or stage a quick little purse search. I'm sure they'd find something interesting enough to put her in a jail cell for the night.

(Not that he would, but I could ask. And just thinking it was possible based on his job that she'd mocked so nastily made me feel better.)

I was still wound-up when I called Bethany—Ms. Dumpster Fire—who I figured was capable of sabotaging the wedding just for kicks. But it turned out she'd taken a baseball bat to her ex-boyfriend's car and was doing a little time in jail already.

And because she'd mouthed off to the prison guards she'd lost her internet and phone privileges for a month, including the days when those emails had been sent.

That meant it was time to confront good old Georgia,

Katie's mom. Not something I was looking forward to. I'd managed to avoid her since the whole Jack Dunner affair, but seems my luck had run out. Good news: at least I was already wearing real pants, so I wouldn't have to change to go see her.

CHAPTER TWENTY-FIVE

I TRACKED GEORGIA DOWN AT THE BUCKIN' BRONC, A dive of a restaurant/bar in Masonville that she seemed to live at. She was perched on a bar stool with some overweight, overdrunk hulk of a man at her side.

"Georgia, have a minute?" I asked, trying not to stare at how bad she looked.

She was my age, for cryin' out loud. But the years had not been kind. If I had to guess, there was probably some meth use involved given the sunken cheeks and bad teeth. What I was seeing was more damage than just booze and cigarettes could do.

She probably wasn't my culprit. The email part was too sneaky. But I had to see it through.

She sneered at me. "Why should I talk to you? You ruined my life. Ruined my baby's life. She had it good until you came along."

I thought about pointing out that when she'd had a kid at fifteen she'd kinda started down that road on her own and that Lucas Dean had started her daughter down the bad road, not me, but that just seemed mean.

(And, hey, look, if you yourself had a kid at fifteen and your life has turned out all sunshine and roses, good for you. Congratulations. Don't read anything into what I just said, okay. I'm snarky sometimes. Especially when forced to confront a woman who could probably take me down with her pinky finger while holding a drink in her other hand.)

Rather than start a fight I knew I couldn't win, I put twenty bucks on the counter. "Because you want some easy money? And a free beer?" I gestured to the bartender.

Georgia eyed the money. I knew she wanted to refuse it and tell me she wasn't going to take money from the likes of me. But money is money and people with principles and empty bank accounts starve. So she took the twenty and shoved it in her bra.

Classy.

I hoped she'd still help, because no way was I going to get that money back, nor would I want it back.

"Where's the beer?" she asked.

The barkeep—an older man who looked like he could take anyone in the place and had the scars on his knuckles to prove it—plopped plastic cups with something resembling beer in front of us and held up two fingers. I handed him a five.

Now I knew why Georgia liked the place so much. Cheap beer.

"Cheers." I took a sip.

Good thing about cheap beer is it's just tasteless whereas cheap alcohol will burn its way right through your esophagus.

"Yeah, for you, maybe. With your family and friends to spend the holiday with. I'm all alone because…"

I cut her off. "Look. Can we get into that some other

time? Right now I'm trying to figure out who's out there sabotaging Jamie's wedding. Was it you?"

She shook her head. "Don't know a thing about it."

"You knew she was getting married, though?"

She shrugged. "You hear things."

I couldn't believe that this sad, decrepit woman had once been one of Jamie's good friends. (In first grade, but still.)

"You don't blame her for Katie and all, do you?"

She inhaled snot up her nose and I tried not to flinch at the sound of it. "Nah. I blame you. You ever get married and something goes wrong there, *that* might be me. Although I'm more likely to let the air out of your tires. But Jamie and I are good. She gave Katie a chance. Tried to look out for her."

Note to self: check tires every time you get into the van because some people are horrible human beings.

"Okay. Thanks." I stood up, but then paused. "You hear anything, will you let me know? There's probably another twenty in it for you."

"Make it fifty."

I thought about bargaining her down, but I'd rather have the information than the money. "Fifty. But only if it's legit."

She grabbed my beer and downed it before I could. "Deal."

I left. One more down. But I was out of suspects and no closer to figuring out who was sabotaging the wedding. I only had four days left and I was at a dead end.

CHAPTER TWENTY-SIX

THE NEXT MORNING ELAINE CALLED ME AND ASKED IF I was up for taking Fancy for a walk with her and Zela. It was still colder out than I'd like but I agreed to meet her in Masonville at noon. She said the high school football field was fenced off and a great impromptu dog park when kids weren't in school.

And she was right. It was perfect. The high school is on a hill above the main road so it has this amazing view in all directions. I took a moment to just stand there and absorb the beauty of those mountains and the crisp blue sky. I don't know what it is, I'm sure some scientist could tell me, but the best blue skies always seem to be when it's a little bit too cold out. Or maybe that's just me.

Elaine and Zela joined us and the two dogs immediately hit it off, all wagging tails and excitement.

I let Fancy off leash and she went tearing through the snow. Zela chased after, making up for her lack of size with an enthusiasm that had her staying hot on Fancy's heels.

"Look at 'em go," I laughed.

"It's so good for Zela to have another dog to run around with." Elaine smiled shyly. "Thank you for meeting us."

"Of course. It's good for Fancy, too. When the barkery was open Fancy had Lulu, that's Jamie's dog, and Hans, that's Greta's dog, to play with. But since it closed a couple months ago I know she's been missing this."

I shivered and stuck my hands in my pockets. I was wearing gloves and an ear warmer, but I was still cold. "Do you know any other dog owners?" I asked.

She shrugged. "Sort of. I know people who own dogs. But not enough to get together with. It'd be weird, wouldn't it, to call someone up and ask for a doggie play date? I mean, other than you, because you offered first." She blushed so much her cheeks turned bright red.

"Yeah, I'm with you on that. I'm not very good at approaching strangers myself. That's what makes having a friend like Jamie so helpful. She'll talk to anyone and drags me right along with her."

"Margaret's kind of like that for me."

I figured anyone who insisted on having their best friend call them Margaret was maybe not so warm and fuzzy, but I let it go.

"Does she have a dog?"

"No." Elaine laughed. "She's not the dog type. I mean some people just don't have dogs, but Margaret is…She could never do the dog hair or the dirt or having to feed them regularly."

I swallowed my thoughts on that one, too. "Well, I do have a dog. And Jamie does. And once all the wedding craziness is over maybe Jamie and Lulu can join us, too, and we'll make this a regular thing. What do you think?"

Elaine bit her lip.

"What?"

"I don't...I mean, Jamie..."

"Because she's marrying Mason? Trust me, she won't find it awkward to be friends with you, Knowing Jamie she's going to make an extra effort to be your friend now that she knows you and Mason have a history."

She crossed her arms tight across her chest. "Is that what people call it these days? A history? Being engaged is having a history?"

I studied her. "Did it upset you when he broke it off?"

"It didn't surprise me. Mason's...Mason. And I'm...me."

"He saw enough in you to ask you to marry him in the first place." I had to duck out of the way as Fancy came barreling right at me, Zela hot on her heels.

"I guess." Elaine kicked at a pile of snow. "I knew I was never good enough for him. But I figured, if he wanted to marry me I'd be a fool to say no."

I grabbed her by the shoulders and looked her in the eyes. "Elaine, I don't know you well. But I've come to know Mason. And he's not a man who'd ask just any woman to marry him. He saw something in you. Something worthy."

"Margaret said he asked because he needed someone who'd keep the books and keep his grandma from pestering him. And that I was perfect for that. I could blend into the background."

"You know, I have to say this Margaret woman sounds like a real..." (I used a word I won't repeat here.)

"No. It's not like that. She's...She knows me. We've been friends since we were babies. She was just telling me the truth so I wouldn't get my expectations up and want more from Mason than I was going to get."

A little hard to argue that he'd cared more for her than

he'd appeared to since he'd dumped her the minute he saw Jamie. But that didn't sound like the kind of best friend I'd want to have. There's the type of friend who tells it to you straight (which I like to think I am) and then there's someone who nastily points out every single flaw or imperfection you have to keep you down (which is what Margaret sounded like to me).

One can be useful, one needs to be removed from your life as soon as humanly possible. But when someone has spent most of their life brainwashed by that kind of Negative Nelly there's no point in coming at things head-on.

"Fair enough. If she kept you from feeling brokenhearted when things ended with Mason, then I guess it worked. But I still think it would be good to be friends with Jamie. Trust me. You'll like her. I'll introduce you to Greta, too."

"Who's Greta?"

"Oh, she was all over the papers a while back for her husband's death. Remember the body they found behind the barkery?"

"She's your friend?"

"She is. And she's a good friend to have. She stepped in when Jamie's wedding dress was ruined. She's a bit of a crazy woman, but I don't know what we would've done without her."

"What happened to Jamie's dress?"

"It was about ten sizes too big. We didn't know anyone who could fix it in time because there was all this custom beading, so Greta found her a different dress to wear."

"Oh."

"What?" I looked at her, wondering if she somehow had a line on my culprit.

"Well, um, I could've probably fixed it for her. I..." She bit her lip. "Don't tell anyone, alright?"

"Tell them what?"

"You know the custom couture hand-beaded wedding dress Margaret supposedly ordered from some Paris designer?"

"Yeah."

"I'm actually the one making it for her."

"Really?"

"Oh, yeah. No one will know the difference."

I raised an eyebrow at that.

"No, really. I..." She blushed. "I'm not good at many things, but I can sew. Really really well."

"But how is she going to use the name of some Paris designer and not get caught?"

"I based it on the woman's designs. When I'm done no one will be able to tell the difference."

"Wow. Well, congratulations on being so good at what you do that you could pull that off. But wouldn't it be better for you if everyone knew it was your work?"

She looked at the ground. "Yeah. But Margaret really wanted to be in the paper and she knew stupid Peter Nielsen wouldn't come to her wedding unless it was newsworthy."

(Peter Nielsen was the sole reporter for *The Baker Valley Gazette*, the only paper in the valley.)

"So she figured a New York chef, a six-foot tall ice sculpture, a Paris couture gown, and a pair of horses would be newsworthy enough to attract him?"

She nodded. "And she was right."

"Are the horses going to really be ponies? Is the chef really from Albuquerque?"

Elaine's eyes filled with tears. "That's not funny."

"I'm sorry, Elaine. I was just teasing. But her, not you."

"I'm getting cold, I better go. Come on, Zela." She whistled Zela to her and left without another word.

I let her go, feeling bad for upsetting her. I hadn't meant anything by it. And, really, didn't she deserve to get the credit for making such an exquisite dress instead of having her hard work passed off as that of someone famous?

CHAPTER TWENTY-SEVEN

THE NEXT DAY GRETA CALLED ME. (I'D GIVEN UP ON EVER playing in another solitaire tournament again I was getting so many calls about the wedding, but I had just sat down to try to sneak in one little game of FreeCell when the phone rang.)

"Hey, Greta, how's it going? All the preparations for the reception coming along?"

"Yes. The food has started to arrive. You should know better Maggie than to let a French chef have an unlimited budget and creative control."

"Why? What's going on?"

"Do you think Jamie and Mason's friends are ready for frog legs and fish eggs and raw beef?"

"Ummm…Hm. Depends on if they know that's what it is. I think they'll probably try anything if it's described in French. I mean pâté certainly sounds better than liver paste, right?"

"Maggie. This is not a joke. This is Jamie's wedding."

"I understand that, Greta. But we were in a bit of a bind. And Jean-Philippe agreed to bail us out on one simple condition—that he be allowed to set the menu. He said he was an artiste and could not be limited."

"That should not have been allowed. You must stand firm with men like that. Give me his number. I will take care of this."

"Um, Greta, we really can't afford to lose our chef three days before the wedding."

"And you will not. I will explain to this man who his audience is and that he must adjust his expectations. No raw meat. That must not happen."

"Well, I can agree with you on that one. And if you think you can bring him around without him quitting in a huff, you are more than welcome to try."

"I will not try, I will succeed."

I gave her his phone number, silently wishing I could be a fly on the wall for that conversation.

"Anything else, Greta?"

"Perhaps. There was an expensive SUV that drove up to my house this morning, but when the security guard walked towards it, the person quickly drove away. He did not get a plate. He thought they must be tourists looking at the different houses in the area. I am not so sure."

"Why?"

"You have been here. People do not come to my house that are not trying to come to my house. And there is no reason for strangers from out of town to try to come here."

"But perhaps our saboteur got wind of all of the food and party items being delivered there and was trying to check it out?"

"Perhaps."

That was a frightening possibility.

"Greta, since when do you have a security guard?"

"Since I agreed to throw this wedding. I will not let

anyone ruin this for Jamie. I have told the guards to shoot anyone who steps on this property without permission."

"Shoot them? Greta, you can't shoot them." That's all we needed. For Greta's house to be off-limits because it was a crime scene. (Again.)

She sighed. "So I was informed."

"Okay. Well, keep an eye out, will you? If that expensive SUV comes back and you can get a plate I'm sure I can convince Matt to run it for me."

"I will. Now I must go."

She hung up. She might be abrupt at times, but I was pretty sure Jamie and I were going to appreciate that efficiency of hers before this was all through.

CHAPTER TWENTY-EIGHT

THAT NIGHT I WORKED MY FINGERS TO THE BONE HELPING my grandpa, Lesley, and Matt put together the decorations for the church.

My grandpa had managed to get his hands on a large assortment of fresh pine boughs, poinsettias, amaryllis, and paperwhites. It gave us a lot to work with, but it was all raw materials. Which meant we had to use twine and wire to turn them into something beautiful.

(And, yes, it would've been better if we could've waited until the night before the wedding to do it all, but there was this little thing called a rehearsal dinner that we were all going to have to attend, so we had soaked everything all day to hydrate it as well as we could and sprayed it with something meant to preserve it as much as possible and were going to store the finished products in the most ideal conditions we could. You work with what you have. And thank your lucky stars that your incredibly rich friend can snap her fingers and procure the type of refrigerators you see at floral boutiques and then have them delivered right to your door and set up in your garage in less than a day.)

Thankfully Lesley was far more artistically inclined than I am, because my results would've looked like a kindergarten project not a professional wedding display without her creative guidance.

And, surprisingly, Matt was amazing at building small wreaths from the pine boughs. I didn't think he'd have it in him, but he did. My grandpa, because of all the work he did with his miniatures, I already knew would be fantastic at it.

I was the problem child. But I managed.

It was actually a really fun night. I liked seeing how my grandpa and Lesley were together even if I was still freaked out by the fact that they were married now. Such a little thing, getting married. One day that if you skipped over it on a Facebook update you'd never even know had happened. But it changed everything. It made it all permanent and important.

I shuddered. How could people believe that that was such a normal progression? Shouldn't dedicating yourself to spending that much of your life with someone be this Herculean decision that was made only in the most extreme circumstances?

And yet people made these decisions all the time. Look at Greta.

Then again, that's kind of how I think of having kids, too. I mean, unless you screw it up, that is a lifelong commitment that doesn't come with the option of divorce. And yet some crazy percentage of kids are not planned. (I just looked it up, it's close to 50%. Think about that...)

But that's why I am what I am and other people are happily married with kids. Because it turns out that sometimes you can't think about things too much or else you'll never do them. You just have to jump on in there and let the hormones set the course. That's how the frickin' species keeps going.

Still.

I think about these things. A lot.

Too much, perhaps.

Perhaps.

Anyway. Fun night. Sore fingers. Beautiful decorations as a result.

CHAPTER TWENTY-NINE

THE NEXT MORNING I HELPED MASON TRANSPORT THE hand-chosen selection of rare wines he wanted to serve at the reception over to Greta's and gave him an update on where we were so far.

"How much does one of those bottles of wine back there cost?" I asked him.

"Depends on the bottle. Anywhere from a couple hundred to a couple thousand."

"Have you met Jamie's sorority sisters? I mean, sure, a few have finely-tuned palates, but the rest? You could give them Two-Buck Chuck and they'd be fine."

He chuckled. "This is my wedding, Maggie. I'm not going to hold back the good wine just because a few people won't appreciate it."

"All I'm saying is if someone walks up to one of the wine-serving stations and asks for their wine by color that you should probably have a stock of some cheaper stuff to serve them. No point in giving someone who wants the 'red' a glass of a thousand-dollar wine."

"Who knows? It might convert them to an appreciation for fine wines."

I snorted. "Not likely. You know I actually went to a wine tasting once. They had Chardonnays. The whole wine tasting, all nine glasses or whatever it was, were Chardonnays."

"And?"

"And the more expensive the glass of wine was, the more quintessentially Chardonnay with its oakiness and butteriness, the less I liked it. It turns out the French Chardonnays were a complete waste where I was concerned."

"Well, Maggie, that's good to know. But maybe not everyone is like that."

"Maybe. I'm just sayin'…Don't go throwing good wine after beer taste buds."

"I'll keep that in mind."

I made sure everything else was looking good at Greta's and that there had been no more sign of the mystery luxury SUV—who it seemed maybe was just a lost tourist—before heading home to confirm the party buses for the reception and make sure that nothing else had slipped through the cracks.

All in all, we were on track. I still didn't know who the culprit was, so I knew there was always a chance of a last-minute mess, but I was feeling good about things. Optimistic.

Of course that was before Fancy and I headed down to Denver to pick up Jean-Philippe from the airport. (He'd insisted that I had to be the one to pick him up. Said he needed the time with me if he was going to be at his best.)

When Matt heard that, he wanted to come with me, but he couldn't because he had to work so he'd have the actual night of the wedding off. I also reminded him that Jean-Philippe was no temptation to me anymore, but to make him feel better about the whole situation, I took Fancy. No way anything untoward was going to happen with Fancy in the van.

It's a long drive—a couple hours each way—but she loves drives. She puts her head right at my shoulder and watches the world go by. Or takes a good long nap.

Plus, I have the whole back of the van fixed up with a giant dog bed, non-spill water bowls, and some chew toys. (Chew toys are a must. My shredded back seatbelt is testament to what happens when a bored dog is stuck traveling too long with nothing to chew on.)

Honestly, it was like puppy nirvana back there. Passengers? What passengers? My dog was my priority.

The drive down was uneventful. It helped that it was a Thursday so there was no real ski traffic, not like on the weekends.

I managed to coordinate my timing with Jean-Philippe so that I only had to circle the airport twice before he arrived in the pick-up area.

Sure, I could've parked in the cellphone lot and waited for him to call, but I prefer that "slow-crawl, don't want to stop and get in trouble with the cops, but don't want to pass through too fast" game that all the cars play.

(Can I just say that airport pick-up and drop-off is one of the most frustratingly stupid things in the world? Do they really think that not allowing cars to stop and wait for a passenger is somehow safer? It's about as useful as telling me

I can't have a half-drunk bottle of Coke and go through the security line at the airport. If I were savvy enough to have liquid explosives in a Coke bottle, I'm pretty sure I'd also be able to get around whatever security controls they have in place. But whatever. The world is impractical and foolish sometimes. It's all about optics after all. It doesn't matter if you are safe as long as you feel safe, right? Right.)

I hopped out of the van and ran around to give Jean-Philippe a quick hug. I have to give it to the man. He was still a looker. Not tall and handsome like Matt, but dark and slender in that European way. And he was short. How had I never noticed that before? Matt was tall enough to be nicely comforting and protective when he gave me a hug, but Jean-Philippe and I were eye-to-eye, which I would've sworn up and down was not my type. But there he was and I'd fallen for it three times.

"Ah, Maggie. So good to see you." He kissed me on each cheek. "I am looking forward to this time with you. You can tell me all about this man you are bringing to the wedding and I will tell you why he is all wrong for you and you should throw him over for me."

He opened the back of the van to store away his bag. Fancy was standing there, filling the entire space. She stepped forward, eager to see who we were picking-up.

He backed up three steps, a hand over his heart like he was about to faint. "What is that beast?"

I laughed and ruffled Fancy's ears. "This is my dog, Fancy. You knew I have a dog. You've seen pictures of her."

"I did not realize she was so enormous. Why would you have a dog this big? Dogs should fit in a purse. You should carry them around with you. They should not be the size of a horse. She could eat a person."

"She's more likely to smother someone with kisses."

Fancy tried to get out of the van to reach him, because she loves all men whether they love her or not, but I shoved her back inside along with his bag and slammed the door.

"Come on. Before the cops come along and tell us to get going." I opened the passenger-side door and ran around to the other side and slid in behind the wheel.

Jean-Philippe hadn't moved.

"Jean-Philippe. If you want me to drive you, you will get in this van now. If you don't, let me know and we can arrange some alternate form of transportation."

He carefully stepped closer to the van. Fancy poked her nose at him through the space between the seat and the window, and he jumped back again.

"Fancy. Back. Give the man a little breathing room." I grabbed her by the collar to keep her out of his way while I rooted around for a handful of treats and threw them in the back. Fancy immediately went after the treats, all thoughts of Jean-Philippe forgotten.

"It's safe now. Don't worry, she's not going to eat you. She probably won't even lick you. She'll just sniff at you a bit."

He got into the car, keeping a wary eye on her the whole time, but Fancy was still sniffing around for every last bit of the treats I'd thrown her. I pulled out and started the drive back home.

Once she finished with the treats, Fancy did snuffle at his hair a bit, but when it was clear he had no interest in petting her she harrumphed and laid down in the back to go to sleep.

"So..." I asked as I merged onto I-70, avoiding all the crazies who'd been caught up in the 225 exit-only lanes, "Ready to cook for a hundred and twenty-five guests?"

"Of course. I am a professional, am I not?"

"And did you and Greta talk about the menu?"

He sniffed. "Yes."

"And everything's good?"

"Yes."

"No raw meat?"

"Beef tartare is a classic. And mine has a perfect yolk on top."

"But you're not going to serve it at Jamie's wedding are you?"

He huffed. "No. I will not serve it at Jamie's wedding. Nor it seems will I serve frog legs. You women do not understand the art that is being a chef. Not being allowed to freely express yourself. But I have spoken to this Greta woman and I understand my audience would not appreciate my art. So I will adjust."

"Good." I gave him my best smile. "I'm glad you're here, Jean-Philippe. We need you."

That seemed to mollify him, which was good, for the most part, except that meant the rest of our conversation centered on Matt and whether or not he really was a good match for me. My conclusion: Yes. Jean-Philippe's: No.

Of course. I wouldn't have expected less.

CHAPTER THIRTY

ONE HOUR AFTER I DROPPED JEAN-PHILIPPE OFF IN Bakerstown, my phone started ringing. And that one-hundred-and-twenty-five-guests number started to climb.

It seemed someone recognized Jean-Philippe. (Or perhaps, knowing Jean-Philippe, he told everyone and their mother who he was.) Whichever way it went down, as soon as word spread that *the* Jean-Philippe Gaston was catering Jamie's wedding all of the locals who'd decided not to come because they had better plans changed their minds. This was, after all, a once-in-a-lifetime opportunity for many of them.

I made a point of telling the first guests who called what I thought of people who change their mind about attending a wedding last-minute, but then one of the guests pointed out to me that Jamie had been the one to change the wedding date on everyone first. If she hadn't done that then there wouldn't have been any confusion about what day it was happening and nobody would've cancelled in the first place.

After that I shut up and told everyone they'd be more

than welcome with a nice, fake smile on my face while silently worrying about just how insane the next two days were going to be.

My phone kept ringing into the night. By the time I finally went to bed at ten o'clock we were up to a hundred and seventy-five guests. And counting.

Good thing Greta's ballroom was big enough to handle that many. The question was, would the chef be willing?

The next morning I found myself very grateful that I don't speak French.

(Well, no more than to say, "Hi, I don't speak French. How much is that thing I'm pointing at?" Or, "Where is this address I'm pointing at on this piece of paper?" I find that learning at least that much of a foreign language before going to a country really helps. It's better than the standard American approach of talking really loudly and slowly in English and somehow expecting a person to magically comprehend a language they never learned.)

Because I didn't actually speak French I didn't know what my very irate French chef was saying so loudly as he paced around Greta's kitchen, banging pots and pans onto various surfaces.

But I was pretty sure all the words flowing out of his mouth were ones I'd never really want to understand. The one or two I recognized from films or books were definitely classified as profanity.

I'd waited to break the news until we were at Greta's because I was hoping the sight of the beautiful commercial kitchen associated with the ballroom would be enough to ease the pain of finding out his guest list had pretty much doubled overnight.

It hadn't helped.

Greta, of course, didn't even bat an eye at my news. She simply waved over a very competent looking young woman who'd been standing off to the side with a clipboard and issued a series of quiet, precise commands while Jean-Philippe screamed and paced and slammed things around.

Greta turned to me. "We will not do a sit down meal. We will have food stations instead. This will make it easier."

Jean-Philippe stared at her in horror and then went back to his shouting.

Greta did an admirable job of ignoring Jean-Philippe's little tantrum until he reached for a stack of fine porcelain plates in the corner, at which point she finally snapped, "Enough."

He stared at her. "You do not understand. There are now twice as many guests. How can I do this? I do not have the food. I do not have the help. I do not..."

She held up her hand and he stopped speaking immediately. That was a trick I needed to learn.

"Write down what you need. Food and people."

"We have only twenty-four hours. How can I...?"

"Write it down."

"But the food. I need..."

"Write it down. There is nowhere in this world that is not a twenty-four hour flight away, no? This is true?"

"Yes."

"Then write it down."

"But the staff..."

"Write. It. Down. Now. Before we have less than twenty-four hours and we actually have a problem." She turned away, shaking her head just enough to show her disgust. "Chefs. Take my advice, Maggie. Never marry one."

"Was one of your husbands a chef?" I asked as Jean-Philippe scribbled furiously.

"Yes. My ninth, I believe. He was Austrian. Great cook. Horrible husband." She glanced back at Jean-Philippe before turning to me. "Have you told Jamie about the increase in the number of guests?"

"No. Crap! The cupcakes."

Greta nodded.

"I can't tell her, Greta. I can't ask her to bake another hundred cupcakes on the eve of her wedding. She has the rehearsal dinner tonight."

Greta patted my arm. "Do not worry. I will see to it."

"How?"

She just smiled. "Do you doubt?"

"You? No."

"Then go. It will be fine."

"Are you sure?" I glanced towards Jean-Philippe.

Greta just stared at me.

"Okay. Jean-Philippe? Will you be okay?" I asked

He was still muttering over his list, but he nodded.

I didn't stick around to ask twice.

CHAPTER THIRTY-ONE

On the way home I decided to swing by the church and see how Luke was doing.

I'd always loved that church. It wasn't big. But it was what I thought the quintessential church should look like. One story, white, with a peaked roof, and the mountains framing it from behind. Inside I knew there were polished wooden pews and a simple altar at the front where the pastor could deliver his sermons. There was a small reception area where people could gather before services and a couple bathrooms and the pastor's office, but that was it: a simple place to come together and pray together.

I was surprised to see Georgia lurking in the parking lot, talking to one of Luke's men.

"Georgia. What brought you to town?"

She flinched at the sound of my voice, but recovered quickly. "Sayin' hi to a friend. You got a problem with that?"

"At the church where Jamie's wedding's going to be held?"

"How'm I supposed to know that? I just needed to see Zeke for a minute."

I looked back and forth between the two of them. Something was definitely up, the question was whether they were conspiring to ruin Jamie's wedding or it was something completely unrelated like a little drug deal between friends.

"I will if something happens with this church to keep Jamie from having her wedding here tomorrow. So keep that in mind."

Georgia hunched her shoulders and turned away from me. "Told you I don't have a problem with her."

"Okay, then."

I started to walk into the church and then turned back. "Oh, and Georgia?"

"Yeah? What?"

"If I come back out to my van and have a flat tire, I'm calling the cops. Got it?"

She sneered at me, but then made a straight line for her beat-up old truck and peeled out of the parking lot. Good enough. I wasn't trying to make friends.

I found Luke in the basement, doing a final walkthrough with the pastor. Luke was good-looking in that laid-back, seedy, let's break a few laws and keep it casual sort of way. It was an interesting contrast to the portly little pastor with his balding head who had to be no more than five-two.

"We all good for tomorrow?" I asked.

Luke nodded. "Sure are, gorgeous. You here to give me a thank-you kiss?"

I ignored him. "Pastor, you agree?"

"I do." He took my hands in his. "And please, tell Mason and Jamie how grateful we are for this. Without their help..." There were tears in his eyes and it made me a little teary, too.

"I will. I'm glad they could help. And I'm sure they are, too."

I squeezed his hands one more time before stepping away. "I better go. I have to check on all the other arrangements before the rehearsal dinner tonight."

I hurried outside. Man, the things I'd do for a friend.

I checked back in with Greta. She'd already procured for Jean-Philippe an additional six prep staff, all qualified enough to meet his exacting standards, and all of the food except for the lobster tails had already arrived or was on its way.

I decided I didn't want to think too closely about what regional events might be missing staff and/or food they were expecting to use the next day.

Money, it can buy pretty much anything if you're willing to use it and know the right people.

CHAPTER THIRTY-TWO

THE REHEARSAL DINNER WAS AT THE COUNTRY CLUB. (Fortunately *that* hadn't been cancelled.) Although it did require me to dress up, which bleh. Of course, it also required Matt dressing up and I have to say he cleaned up very nicely indeed. I had myself one very attractive boyfriend who somehow made all the mess of looking pretty feel worth it.

We were two of the first guests to arrive so we found Mason and Jamie huddled together in the entryway chuckling about something on his phone.

"What's so funny," I asked.

Jamie showed me the phone. There was a text on it that read, "Hey baby. Thank you so much for last night." And below that another one, "I'm going to miss you when you get married. Maybe we can still keep in touch after?" and then a series of emojis.

"Who texts somebody an eggplant?" I asked.

All three of them looked at me like I'd said something really stupid.

"What? What did I say?"

Matt just kissed me on the cheek. "There are so many reasons I love you. Just when I think you are the smartest woman I know you say something like that. It's adorable."

"I don't want to be adorable. I want to understand what I'm missing."

Jamie quickly explained what the series of little images at the end of the message meant. At which point I blushed bright scarlet. "What? Are you serious?"

She nodded.

"Who…?" And then it finally dawned on me that we were looking at Mason's phone. On the eve of his wedding. "Who sent these, Mason? Who is thanking you for last night? On the eve of your wedding?"

He smiled a little smugly. "Someone who clearly didn't check to see how I spent last night before sending those messages."

Jamie grinned at me. "You want me to explain that one, too?"

"Oh shut up. I got that one, thanks. So…Some random stranger sent you text messages to make it look like you were having an affair. But you know you're not. So what good does that do them?"

Jamie handed Mason back his phone as his parents walked in the door. He walked over to greet them while Jamie answered my question. "Whoever it was called Mason's phone and asked for me, supposedly because they couldn't reach me on my phone. And while they were chatting with me about my customer satisfaction with my wedding dress," she raised an eyebrow at that one, "the text messages came in."

"Ah. I get it. So someone made sure you'd see them."

"Umhm. Seems they thought I'd believe them and call off the wedding last-minute over my cheating fiancé."

"But they messed up by mentioning last night."

Jamie laughed. "No, they messed up by thinking I would ever believe something like that of Mason. And, honestly, do you think Mason would ever get involved with a woman who uses emojis?"

I looked over at the man who stood with perfect posture in a conservatively cut expensive suit, put together from head to toe. "Good point. So that attempt failed."

"Yes it did." Jamie beamed a smile at us before walking over to kiss Mason's cheek and loop her arm through his.

Matt put an arm around my shoulders. I leaned into him. "You know what this means, don't you?"

He nodded. "Someone's still trying to ruin this wedding."

"I hope that was their last try, but I'm afraid it wasn't." I told him about seeing Georgia at the church earlier that day. "It might've just been two friends talking, but given what's been happening…"

He nodded. "I'll have Ben run by the church a couple times tonight, just in case. He's on duty and I'm sure he won't mind doing it for Jamie's sake."

"Thanks." I was ready for this wedding to be over. Not that I didn't want my friend to have her happy day, but it was stressful constantly trying to think about how else things might go wrong or scrambling to fix them last-minute.

CHAPTER THIRTY-THREE

THE MORNING OF JAMIE'S WEDDING DAWNED COLD AND clear and beautiful. For a brief moment, I let myself believe the worst had passed and we were fine. I was even smiling as I walked Fancy down the icy streets of Creek.

But then my phone rang.

It was the pastor's wife. Telling me that he was violently ill and wouldn't be able to complete the ceremony that day.

Coincidence? I doubted it.

As soon as I dropped Fancy off at home, I drove to their house.

(I know. How rude. The man was too sick to officiate a wedding and there I was at eight in the morning on his doorstep, knocking loudly. But I hoped our little saboteur had finally slipped up.)

"Ms. Carver? What are you doing here?" The pastor's wife was a very friendly, plump, older woman who I'd never actually seen be rude or mean to anyone ever. So even though she probably wanted to tell me to go away, she didn't.

"I need to know everything the pastor ate in the last twenty-four hours."

She lifted her chin. "I didn't tell you he was sick to his stomach. I just said he was unwell."

"But he is, right? Like food poisoning kind of sick?"

She sniffed like the very topic was offensive to her. "Yes."

"I think someone put something in his food."

"What? No. Who would do such a thing?"

"The same person who'd turn off the furnace in a church in the hopes that the pipes would burst so no one could get married there."

"Oh, this is horrible. What is the world coming to?" She waved me inside and led me to the kitchen. "Well, it can't be anything I ate or I'd be sick, too, right?"

"Right. Probably."

She glanced around with a big sigh. There were tins of food everywhere. "It had to be this time of year, didn't it?"

"Is this all from your parishioners?"

She nodded. "They know we don't like to receive money, so they try to feed us. Unfortunately, Pastor Nelson has a bit of a sweet tooth."

"Well, let me see what I can find." I started making my way through the various stacks of food everywhere. Some were still sealed, so those were easy to eliminate. There were also some that she swore he'd never eat and some that they'd both tried the day before.

That left a stack of about fifteen various plates and tins.

I looked through each one, but none of the names were familiar. Not until I reached the last one.

"Elaine Parks is a parishioner of yours?"

"Oh, yes. She's an absolute sweetheart. Such a help."

"And he ate one of these?"

"Of course. They're Jerry's favorite. He had at least

three of them yesterday even though I told him they'd ruin his appetite." She blinked. "You can't possibly think Elaine..."

"She was engaged to Mason at one point, wasn't she?"

"But Elaine? No. It couldn't be. She's too nice."

I held up the plate of chocolate brownies. "She's the only one whose name I recognized...Do you have her home address?"

"I really..."

"I'll get it from Mason if I don't get it from you."

She lifted her chin. "Then do that. Because she couldn't possibly have done this."

"Fine. But I'd suggest you throw those brownies out."

"Oh, I couldn't. They're his favorite."

"Look, lady. Something here made your husband horribly sick. Honestly, you should probably throw it all out just to be safe."

She stared around the room. "But, there's so much."

"Your tummy, not mine. Will the church be ready at four?"

"I told you, Pastor Nelson can't do the service."

"But we can still use the church can't we?"

She pressed her lips together. "Who will officiate?"

"I'll figure it out. Just have the church ready, please."

"It's a house of God."

"And we'll respect that. Do you really want to reward this person for sabotaging your church and poisoning your husband?"

She thought about it for a long moment and finally shook her head. "No. You can use the church."

"Thank you."

I called Matt as I walked to the car. "Hey, Maggie. What's wrong?"

"I think Elaine poisoned the pastor."

"Elaine? No."

I filled him in on what I'd found.

"I still can't believe it."

"Yeah, neither could the pastor's wife. But he's puking his guts out and had at least three of those brownies yesterday and I didn't recognize any of the other names, so...I think I better check it out."

"I'll meet you there."

"No, that's fine. She's harmless. I need you to do something else for me."

"Sure. Anything."

"Research who has to officiate a wedding in Colorado. I seem to think you can just do it yourselves, but I need that confirmed. And if that is the case then call my grandpa and ask him if he's willing to lead the ceremony."

"Couldn't Mason have one of his judge friends do it?"

"Probably. But at this point, I'm keeping everything in the family where I can control it."

"Okay. Will do. But, Maggie?"

"Yeah?"

"Please don't actually kill Elaine. I'd rather not have to date a woman who's in prison."

"Haha. Funny."

"I wasn't kidding, Maggie."

I rolled my eyes. "Fine. I won't kill her. I'll just put the fear of me in her so she doesn't do anything else to screw up this wedding."

"Maggie..."

"Look, I'm not going to do anything to get myself arrested, alright? But I am going to have a little chat with that woman about why she's doing this and tell her to knock it off. Good enough?"

"Good enough."

I hung up and called Mason. He wanted to know why I needed Elaine's address the morning of his wedding, but I told him he didn't need to know and he was smart enough not to press me on it.

CHAPTER THIRTY-FOUR

ELAINE LIVED IN A SURPRISINGLY TIDY CABIN JUST OUTSIDE of Bakerstown. As I drove up I could see Zela outside barking, but no sign of Elaine. Zela was agitated and ridiculously happy to see me. She kept circling my legs as I walked from the front gate to the door, barking at me.

I stopped to try to calm her, but she just kept barking and circling. I did manage to touch her coat as she circled. She'd been outside a while. Not enough to freeze, thankfully. I remembered Elaine talking about the heated dog house she'd bought her.

Clearly something was wrong. Elaine might be the type of person to try to ruin her ex's wedding, but she didn't strike me as the type of person to harm her dog.

I knocked on the front door. No answer.

I knocked again. Still no answer.

I thought about walking around the perimeter and peeking inside, but I had a wedding to get to and a saboteur to confront, so instead I tried the doorknob. It turned. Her house was unlocked.

(Don't tell anyone, but my grandpa's house always is, too. In the mountains you don't expect trouble.)

Before I could debate how smart it was to walk into someone's house uninvited (my prior experiences doing so hadn't always gone so well), Zela pushed past me and ran inside. Her bark changed. It was the "someone get in here now there's a problem" bark.

I wanted to follow her, but I knew I probably shouldn't.

I called Matt.

"Hey, Maggie. What's up?"

"I'm at Elaine's. Something is off. Her dog was locked outside and going nuts. I tried the front door and the dog ran inside and is now sounding very alarmed. I'm going in."

"Maggie. Wait for a cop to get there."

"I can't, Matt. But you can stay on the line with me. That way if something happens, you'll know."

"At least let me call someone."

"I'm going in now. You can hang up and call someone or you can stay on the line and make sure I'm safe. Your call."

"Maggie," he growled at me, but he stayed on the line as I eased inside.

"Elaine? It's Maggie Carver. Are you here?"

The door opened onto a small kitchen that looked like it had come straight out of the sixties. There was a little metal table pressed up against one wall with a peeling laminate top and an old white and pink fridge next to it with the curved lines of that long-ago decade.

On the counter sat a container of cocoa right alongside a bottle of syrup of ipecac.

That'd do it.

"Maggie? Talk to me. Are you okay?" Matt asked.

"I'm fine. I haven't found Elaine yet. The dog's barking

143

in the other room. But there's a bottle of ipecac in the kitchen right next to a container of cocoa."

"Really?"

"Yeah." A little too obvious, if you asked me. I stepped towards the doorway from the kitchen to the rest of the cabin. "Elaine? Are you here?"

There was a small living area divided in two. One side barely fit a recliner and a small television set atop a bookcase. The other side was dedicated to three different sewing machines as well as a workspace for prepping. A dressmaker's dummy stood in the corner, empty. A loft area above appeared to have a small bed.

But Zela was standing at another door, barking. I assumed that one had to be the bathroom. (I hoped for Elaine's sake it was. If not, that meant she had to use an outhouse and well, I wouldn't wish that on anyone, not even the person who might've tried to sabotage my best friend's wedding.)

"Matt, this doesn't look good...." I approached the door.

"What are you seeing?"

"Zela's stopped outside a door. I have to assume it's for a bathroom. If Elaine's in there, she's not responding. Do you want me to wait until a cop gets here?"

"No. Open the door. We need to know what we're dealing with."

"Okay." I turned the handle, trembling. As angry as I was with Elaine for what she'd done, I really wanted her to be okay. I'd seen enough dead bodies for a lifetime.

Zela shoved through the door as soon as she could. The barking stopped, but that was almost worse, because it was replaced with low-level whining. I couldn't move the door more than about eight inches, but it was enough to get my head in for a peek.

Elaine was on the floor, eyes closed, breaths shallow. There was a note next to her. It was printed off of a computer. It said, "I'm sorry. I had to do it."

Really?

"Maggie?" Matt interrupted my thoughts.

"Call an ambulance. Elaine's down. She's still alive, but you need to get someone here as soon as you can."

I hung up on him. I needed to think.

CHAPTER THIRTY-FIVE

WHILE I WAITED FOR THE AMBULANCE AND COPS TO arrive, I turned back to Elaine's living room. There was something that was bugging me about it, but I couldn't figure out what. I slowly walked around the room, looking at everything I saw, trying to figure out what was so off.

(I know. You probably think I should've shoved my way into the bathroom. Problem is, I don't know CPR. So there was nothing useful I could do except probably crack her ribs. Plus, emergency response in the valley is really fast. I figured it'd only be a minute or two before the paramedics were there and they could do a much better job of things than I could.)

Almost every surface had something homemade. There were doilies on the bookcase, mostly crocheted, a few tatted. There were cross-stitches in frames on the walls. And perhaps a water color as well. I saw a small ledger next to the recliner and flipped through the pages without really reading them. It looked like detailed handwritten lists of supplies she'd bought for various craft projects.

The bed, what I could see of it from where I stood, was

neat and tidy. Me if I'd had a bed in a loft I'd never make it because the risk of hitting my head on the ceiling would outweigh my desire for tidiness.

Maybe that was it. Maybe that was what was bugging me.

Everything was put away. There wasn't mail lying around or dirty clothes thrown anywhere. Everything had its place. And was in its place.

So why would Elaine leave the ipecac syrup and cocoa on the counter? If she'd taken the brownies to the pastor, she would've cleaned up first. There weren't any dirty dishes in the sink. So why were those two ingredients out on her counter?

And would a woman who hand-crafted seemingly everything, including her own wardrobe from what I could tell, really print out a suicide note on a computer?

No.

It didn't make any sense.

Just as I reached that conclusion the paramedics came barging in and I was swept out of the way while they managed to get the bathroom door removed.

"She's alive. Barely. Let's get her out of here."

As the paramedics worked to put her on a gurney, a cop who'd arrived in the meantime asked me if I knew what she'd taken.

"No idea. I'm sorry. I don't think she took it deliberately, whatever it was."

"What do you mean?"

I walked him through the whole "this doesn't fit" theory I'd developed. He clearly wasn't buying it.

"Look. Just, humor me a bit, please. And treat this like a potential murder instead of an obvious suicide attempt. My boyfriend, Matt Barnes, he'll vouch for me."

"Oh. You're Matt's girl, huh?"

"Maggie Carver."

He didn't look any more convinced than he had before and I wondered what exactly Matt had been saying about me at work. (Or, more likely, he was basing all his opinions of me on that slam piece Peter Nielsen wrote that cast both me and the police department in a very bad light.)

"Just…Maybe make sure no one can get to her for a few hours at least?" I asked.

"That we can do. Now come on. You can't stay here." He radioed in his status as we walked outside. "The dog hers?"

Zela had followed the paramedics to their vehicle and was barking loudly as she tried to get around them to reach Elaine.

"Yes."

"Then I'll call animal control."

"No. Don't. I'll take her."

One of my worst fears has always been something happening to me and then Fancy being left alone with no one to care for her. No way I was going to let that happen to Zela if I could help it.

"It's protocol, ma'am."

"Just let me take her, please?"

He hesitated for another minute, but finally nodded. "Fine. Take her. But if something goes wrong…"

"Understood. She'll be in the best of hands, I promise." I glanced towards the house. "But can I go back in real quick and grab her food and toys and things?"

"Yes." He didn't look happy, but as long as he let me do it I really didn't care.

I grabbed up the food and some toys and treats. I was tempted to grab the bottle of ipecac, too, but I figured it either didn't have any prints on it at all or the only prints were going to be Elaine's since it was so obviously a plant by whoever had done this.

Although I was still no closer to knowing who that was. I had five hours until the wedding ceremony was supposed to start and I was at square one.

Actually, I was at *less* than square one.

CHAPTER THIRTY-SIX

ZELA BARKED THE WHOLE WAY TO MY HOUSE, BUT SHE calmed down when I finally got her inside and she saw Fancy. They tore through the house and into the backyard. Ah, to be a dog whose only concerns were food, sleep, and play.

I hoped Ms. White would be okay watching three dogs instead of two (she was also watching Lulu for the night). I'm sure she would once she understood the circumstances.

My grandpa crossed his arms and glared at me. "Well? Where'd you go this morning? We have ten minutes until we're supposed to meet at the church and put up all the decorations. I told you I'd help, Maggie, I didn't say Lesley and I would do all the work."

"I know. I'm sorry. I will be there to help."

"What about the dogs? You're just going to leave a strange dog in my house?"

I rubbed the back of my neck. "I hadn't even thought of it, honestly. Maybe she can come with us."

"Maggie."

"I'm sorry, Grandpa, but things have been moving fast

this morning." I explained to him everything that had happened since the pastor's wife called. "I didn't even eat breakfast. I just ran out of here to see if I could figure out who'd done this. And now I need to call them again to see if Elaine actually brought over those brownies or not. And I need to call Mason to see if she has any family that need to know she's in the hospital. And…"

"You need to eat."

"That, too."

"I'll make you a sandwich while you call the pastor and Mason."

"But the church…"

"We can be a few minutes late. It's going to be a long day and you need to eat."

I gave him a quick kiss on the cheek. "Thank you."

He just grunted, but he did go to the kitchen and start fixing me up a roast beef sandwich with Swiss cheese. He even threw in a dill pickle and a handful of chips.

I called Mason first. I hated to tell him about Elaine on the morning of his wedding, but I had to know if she had family.

She didn't. None he'd ever met. And the closest she came to friends was Margaret Kepper who not only was getting married that day, too, but had also sounded like a bit of a bully to me.

"I can run by there," Mason said.

"No. It's your wedding day. Just focus on that."

"Jamie would understand."

"Oh, I'm sure she would. But you can't tell her about this."

"Why not?"

I sighed. "Because the fact that Elaine's in the hospital and the pastor was poisoned means that whoever this is who's trying to ruin your wedding is officially dangerous. I don't want that hanging over her head today."

"Shouldn't she know? In case whoever it is comes after her?"

"Good point. Fine. I'll tell her." She was at her mom's in honor of tradition.

"Did you just say that the pastor was poisoned?"

"Yes. Syrup of ipecac. He can't do the ceremony."

"So who is going to do the ceremony then?"

I tensed. "My grandpa will."

There was a long silence on the other end of the line.

"Maggie, you do understand that my family is one of the most prominent families in the valley, don't you?"

"Yes. And?" I sat back, just waiting for it.

"So there will be judges and lawyers and doctors and other upstanding members of society there?"

"Yeees."

"And your grandpa…"

"Has a colorful history?"

"That's one way to put it."

"Mason."

"Yes, Maggie?"

"Did I make this thing happen? Even though I hate weddings and only had ten days to do it in?"

"Yes."

"And are you seriously going to tell me now that my solution to your latest issue isn't good enough for you? That my *family* isn't good enough for you?"

Another long pause.

"Well, are you? Because as much as I love Jamie and want this day to work out for her, I can wash my hands of this whole mess right now. Instead of me and my grandpa spending the next hour or more at the church decorating it for *your* wedding we can just sit at home and play Scrabble."

"You wouldn't do that to Jamie."

"No, I wouldn't. Lucky for you. Now. Do I need to tell my grandpa you don't think he's good enough to lead the ceremony?"

He sighed. "No. It's fine. As long as Jamie and I end this day a married couple and everyone comes out of it alive, I'll be happy."

"Good man. I'll see you at the church. "

I hung up.

Yes, I had badgered the groom into accepting my less-than-perfect solution to the pastor problem, but I did not care. I could rely on my grandpa. No one was going to take him out before the ceremony even if someone were inclined to try. Mason might prefer some chichi judge to preside, but I wasn't taking chances at that point.

Jamie was my next call. "Maggie! Can you believe it's the big day?"

I forced myself to sound cheerful. "No. Time flies."

"Greta just arrived with the dress and it's so exquisite. And the hair and makeup ladies are here and we're drinking champagne and…"

"Don't drink too much champagne, okay? Remember, you have to walk down an aisle with close to two hundred people watching you."

"I won't. Just a bit to take the edge off. I'm so excited!"

"And I'm excited for you."

"Then why aren't you here?"

"Because someone needs to put up all the decorations in

the church and I can't just ask my grandpa and Matt to do that. It wouldn't be fair."

"But your hair and makeup."

"It'll be fine. I'll try to swing by after. Save me champagne."

"I will. You know, it could be you next…"

"No. No, no, no. We are not going there today. That topic is off-limits as of now. Look. I have to go, but I called for a reason."

She was immediately serious. "What is it?"

I filled her in on what had happened that morning. "I've got it handled, okay? My grandpa will step in to lead the ceremony and you guys can self-solemnize."

"What?"

"It sounds dirty, but it just means you sign the wedding certificate instead of the pastor. I had Matt look it up this morning and he texted me a link. You'll be fine. You're still getting married today. But I called because I need you to be careful. Don't trust anyone."

"But I thought you said Elaine was the one who gave the pastor the brownies?"

"Eh. That's what someone wanted us to think, but no. It was too easy."

"So who was it?"

"I don't know. Could be a couple people. Just be careful, and…check the tires on your car before you leave the house, okay?"

"The tires on my car?"

"Something Georgia said to me. Just channel a little bit of me today, alright? Question first, trust second."

"Okay. Fine. I will. But promise you'll try to swing by for hair and makeup?"

"I'll try."

That left one final call to the pastor's wife. She confirmed that Elaine hadn't given them the brownies directly. They'd been left at his office at the church the day before. Which led me to make one more call.

"This is Georgia. What do you want?"

"Hi, Georgia, it's Maggie."

"What do you want?"

"Any chance you were at the church yesterday to drop off some brownies?"

Silence.

"Georgia, Elaine is in the hospital. She may not make it. Now I can either call the cops and tell them you're the one responsible and you can spend New Year's Eve in jail for attempted murder..."

"What? I didn't try to kill no one. What do you take me for?"

"Those brownies? They had syrup of ipecac in them. The pastor has been sick all morning. Did you do that?"

"No."

"But you know who did."

"Not really."

I pinched the bridge of my nose. "What does that mean?"

"Some guy I didn't know came into the Buckin' Bronc and offered me twenty bucks to drop those brownies off at the church."

I quietly banged my head against the wall. "I offered you fifty for any information that might be related to whoever was sabotaging Jamie's wedding."

"I know. That's why I told him I wouldn't do it for less than a hundred."

Of course she had.

"What did this guy look like?"

"Rich."

"Height? Weight? Hair color? Age? Eye color?"

"I don't know. He drove some fancy SUV. Wore sunglasses. Wasn't really memorable otherwise."

"Okay. Fine. And, Georgia?"

"Yeah?"

"Next time someone counters my offer, give me a chance to outbid them, would ya?"

"Will do."

I hung up, wolfed down the sandwich my grandpa had made me, and was at the church only ten minutes late.

(I left Zela and Fancy at the house. They were already fast asleep in the living room by the time I went to leave and I couldn't imagine them getting into trouble in the hour we'd be gone.)

CHAPTER THIRTY-SEVEN

THIRTY MINUTES AFTER I ARRIVED AT THE CHURCH, MY phone rang. It was Georgia.

"Hey Georgia, what's up?"

"That fancy man?"

"Yeah?"

"He came back. Offered me a hundred bucks to do a job for him."

"What job?"

"I don't know. I said I had to call you for a counteroffer. He ran out of here as soon as I reached for my phone."

"You get a better description of him this time around?"

"Still looked rich."

"And?"

I could almost hear her shrug through the phone. "Not young. Not old. Dark hair. A little taller than me."

"Happen to get a plate on that SUV he was driving?"

"No." The way she said it made it sound like the most absurd suggestion she'd ever heard.

"Okay, thanks."

I hung up.

"Who was that?" Matt asked.

I told him about the call. "So I guess keep an eye out for a fancy SUV. And some average-looking rich guy."

"Any idea who it could be?"

"None. I mean, Jamie's dated a few average-looking rich guys over the years, but none that would want to ruin her wedding this bad. Plus, this has to be a local, doesn't it? I mean, who else would know about Elaine and her brownies? Or be able to spread the rumor that the wedding was cancelled? Or know to track down Georgia to have her be the one to deliver the brownies?"

My grandpa joined us. "All good questions. But they won't get the rest of these garlands hung. Now get back to work."

"Yes, sir."

I didn't want to leave when we were done. It looked so nice and I was worried what might happen in the hour until the ceremony started, but I needed to get dressed and check on Fancy and Zela. Plus I had to talk my grandpa into wearing the tuxedo Greta had sent over when I called to tell her about the latest developments. We'd both agreed jeans and flannel shirts were fine for day-to-day wear but not for standing in front of the county's finest leading a wedding ceremony.

My grandpa surprised me. I thought he'd fight me on the tux, but when we got home and I pulled it out of the clothing bag his only concern was whether it would fit well enough for it to look good on him.

(It did. I'd never seen him look so dapper. And unlike some men who can only look comfortable in one type of clothes, he looked just as put together and in control in the tux as he did in his jeans and flannel shirt. Character shows through.)

I was the one who wanted to throw a fit about my outfit.

The bridesmaids' dresses Jamie had chosen were pastel pink. Floofy pastel pink. I looked like someone had stuck a big bunch of cotton candy around my thighs. For a moment there I kind of wished someone had sabotaged the brides-maids' dresses, too. I would've been far happier in that gorgeous blue gown I'd tried on at Greta's.

But Jamie was my best friend. So if I had to spend a day looking all soft and pretty, I'd do it, with a smile.

I glanced at the clock. I had just enough time to run over to her place to get my hair and makeup done by the profes-sionals. (One of the great parts of living in a small town. Everyone who lives in the town is only five minutes away, maybe ten at the most.)

"You okay, Grandpa?" I asked.

"I'll be fine. Where are you headed?"

"To Jamie's. She has someone there to do everyone's hair and makeup."

"Good idea." He glanced at my feet. "I assume you have different shoes to wear at the actual ceremony?"

I laughed. "Yes. No snow boots for the actual walk down the aisle. Although they are more comfortable…"

Ms. White arrived with Lulu as I was racing to my van. I gave her a quick wave and winced as I realized my grandpa was going to be stuck explaining to her the extra house guest. Hopefully she'd be okay with it. If not, the wedding might just end up with a few extra canine guests.

I don't know what instinct made me decide to go the extra block out of the way that would take me by the church on the way to Jamie's house, but I'm glad I did. Because there was a fancy SUV parked in the back corner of the parking lot. One I certainly didn't recognize.

I pulled my van up behind it and jumped out.

(Yes, I know. Stupid. The minute I saw the SUV I should've called the cops. Whoever was trying to sabotage Jamie's wedding had already proven themselves to be dangerous. The last thing I needed to be doing was try to confront them on my own. But it seems my adrenaline reaction is always fight over flight. So I charged on in.)

Good thing I did, though. I barged through the back door of the church and right into a man with two gas cans at his feet. He must've just arrived and paused to assess his surroundings.

"What are you doing?" I asked. (Throwing in a few cuss words for good measure.) "This is a church. Were you really going to burn it down?"

"Get out of my way," he growled.

"No. This is over. Who are you? Why are you trying to ruin my friend's wedding? And what is wrong with you that you'd desecrate a church? And hurt a poor innocent girl with no friends?"

"What are you talking about?"

"Elaine? You poisoned her. And the pastor. Who poisons a pastor?"

"I didn't poison a pastor."

"You didn't pay Georgia to deliver brownies to the pastor yesterday?"

He paused to think about it. "Yeah, I did that."

"Well, those brownies were poisoned. And I found the woman who supposedly made them unconscious on her bathroom floor this morning."

"That wasn't me. I just paid the lady to deliver them."

"But this is." I gestured towards the gas cans.

Reminded of the gas cans, he tried to lunge for one, but I got in the way. It cost me a hard shove into the wall, which hurt like no one's business, but at least he didn't get his hands on the gasoline.

He pushed past me and out the back door before I could stop him and maneuvered the SUV around my van by pulling onto the church lawn.

I immediately called it in to the cops. And, unlike Georgia, I had a license plate to give them. As soon as I gave them that information I also called Matt to tell him what had happened. He promised he'd call the police station and make sure every cop in the area was looking for the guy. He also told me he was dressed and ready and would head to the church so I could go meet up with Jamie.

We weren't going to take any more chances at that point.

CHAPTER THIRTY-EIGHT

JAMIE AND THE OTHER BRIDESMAIDS WERE ALL GIGGLES when I arrived. Clearly they had been enjoying the champagne a little more than necessary. But I told myself that was good. You should be all happy, bubbly on your wedding day.

Caroline looked me up and down. "Maggie, how is it that you can make any outfit look like trash?"

I gave her my best smile. "It's a special skill. I've been practicing it for years."

I took the glass of champagne from Jamie and downed it in one go. "Where are the hair and makeup crew that'll magically transform me into something presentable?"

"Right through here. And don't listen to Caroline, she's just jealous because you always look good even when you look bad."

I tried to parse that one and decided it wasn't worth the effort. I was pretty sure it was meant to be a compliment and that's what counted.

I sat down in the torture chair, closed my eyes, and let

162

the ladies get to work with their hairsprays and blushes and eyeliners and hair pins.

"You're such a treat to work on," the makeup lady whispered. "You just sit there so perfectly."

"That's because I've gone to my happy place so I won't think too much about what you're doing to me. It's what I do when I go to the dentist, too."

She trilled in laughter, but I was serious. It is what I do at the dentist and when someone is intent on turning my hair into a shellacked mess that can stand up on its own.

Jamie leaned close as they were putting on the finishing touches. "Anything else happen that I should know about?"

"Nope. You just focus on the fact that you're about to marry the man of your dreams."

She beamed at me. She was so happy she was almost glowing. "I am, aren't I?"

My phone started to ring just as one of the other bridesmaids ran into the room and pulled Jamie away.

"Hey, Matt. Did you get him?"

"We did."

"And? Who is he? Why is he doing this?"

"His name is Johnny Tinson."

"Tinson? That sounds familiar." But it didn't sound like someone Jamie had dated. "Hey, wait. I know where I heard that before. There's a Bobby Tinson getting married today to Margaret Kepper. That makes total sense."

"What does?"

"He must be the groom's brother or something."

"And? Why does that make sense?"

"Because I bet she was jealous when Jamie moved the wedding. I bet it ruined all her big plans to be the center of attention. Mason's family is a big deal around these parts.

People probably cancelled on her when Jamie moved the wedding. So she thought if she could ruin Jamie's wedding she'd get all the attention again. And the newspaper coverage."

"You really think someone would poison a pastor, almost kill a woman, and try to burn down a church just because they were upset that someone had stolen their limelight?"

"Yeah, from everything Elaine said, I do. Are you going to pick them up?"

"Who?"

"Margaret and Bobby."

"We have no proof they did anything wrong. And it's their wedding day."

"I don't care, Matt. You have to pick them up. If you don't they'll keep trying to ruin Jamie's wedding."

"Maybe not. Maybe it's too late at this point. Maybe they'll just focus on their own wedding."

"I doubt it."

"We have nothing to charge Johnny with, let alone Bobby or Margaret."

"Georgia saw Johnny."

"Georgia is Georgia. Not the best witness."

"I saw him, too. At the church with gas cans."

"But what did you see? A man standing in the back of a church with some gas cans near him."

"Matt, I know this is our guy."

"But there's no way to prove it."

"Matt…"

"Maggie, I serve the law. And the law protects people's rights. Innocent until proven guilty. And we have no proof here."

Jamie came back into the room. "Are you ready? It's time to get to the church."

"Yeah, I'm ready. Gotta go, Matt." I hung up on him.

I really hoped he was right and that it was all over. But I didn't believe that. I would've been much happier if he'd just agreed to arrest everyone instead of being all ethical about it.

CHAPTER THIRTY-NINE

WE WERE ALL WALKING OUT OF JAMIE'S HOUSE, READY TO pile into the limo her father had rented for the drive to and from the church and reception when my phone rang again.

This time it was Mason. I glanced at the limo and then at my phone. "You guys go ahead. I can drive the van over."

"Are you sure?" Jamie asked.

"Yeah. I better take this. And I don't want to hold you guys up. Go."

They piled into the limo, Jamie with her princess dress and the other bridesmaids in their pink cotton candy floof, giggling and talking non-stop about the reception. To be honest, I was kind of glad Mason had given me an excuse to avoid cramming myself into a small contained space with that much estrogen.

Don't get me wrong. I have a few very close female friends that I wouldn't trade away for the world. But surround me with a group of girls packed together like that, especially a giddy group of girls? I'm ready to run.

"Mason. What's up?" I asked, heading towards my van.

"We have a big problem."

I wanted to bury my face in my hands but I couldn't because of all the stupid makeup on my face. "What now?"

"Someone dumped a bunch of hay bales all over the road that leads from my house to the church. It's going to take at least an hour or two to clear them."

"They're just hay bales."

"It's a mess, Maggie. Will you tell Jamie? I'm going to be there, but it might be a while."

I shook my head. "No. Not acceptable. Be more creative."

"What?"

"You need to be more creative about solving this problem. Can you go around it?"

"Not in the limo."

"Mason...What about in a truck?"

"Too snowy."

I was starting to get annoyed. "What about on a snowmobile?"

"I..." He paused. "That might work. But then..."

"Just get around the hay bales. I'll have Matt take care of the rest."

I hung up on him. Not nice, I know, but I was running low on patience by that time and anyone who wasn't a part of the solution was a part of the problem. I called Matt and explained to him what had happened. "Can you send someone to pick up Mason and whoever else is with him? I assume it's his groomsmen. So maybe six people?"

"I'll call Jack."

"Jack? Are you sure?"

"Unless you want me to abandon the church to go get Mason. Or you want to send your grandpa off to do it."

I took a deep breath. "No. That's fine. Send Jack. Thank you."

"Are you headed this way?"

"No. I have something to take care of first."

"Maggie…"

I hung up on him, too.

CHAPTER FORTY

I USED MY PHONE TO FIGURE OUT WHERE MARGARET Kepper's father's farm was located and headed in that direction. I figured I had a few minutes to spare before the wedding started and it was time to end this thing once and for all. The article I found on the farm included a picture of Kepper. She wasn't an attractive woman, not by conventional standards. Her teeth were bizarrely prominent. But she was well-polished, so I'm sure most people saw her as respectable and likeable.

Not me. She was slime in my book and I was determined to let her have it.

Of course, if there's one lesson I keep having to learn over and over again in life, it's this one: Do not act out of anger.

My first car accident when I was sixteen-years-old, I gunned the car to clear an intersection where I was taking a left turn because I was angry at someone who'd just run what I thought was a red light for leaving me hanging out there in the intersection. Unfortunately for me and my temper and the driver of the car behind him, a second car went through the light and I smacked right into him.

I should know by now that acting out of anger is a very bad idea.

And yet…

That's exactly what I did when I drove over to the Kepper Family Farm.

Fortunately for me, there was a guard on the gate who refused to let me through. And my boyfriend knows me far too well. A police cruiser pulled up about a minute after I did. Officer Ben Clark was driving, Matt was in the passenger seat, and somebody was in the back, but I couldn't see who.

Matt got out. "Maggie…"

"I'm tired of this, Matt. It has to end. Now."

"And it will." He turned to the guard on the gate. "Are Ms. Margaret Kepper and Mr. Bobby Tinson on the ranch?"

The guard nodded.

Matt opened the back door of the SUV and pulled out the guy from the church. He perp-walked him over to the gate guard and then released him.

"Let me make this clear. I think this man here along with Margaret Kepper and Bobby Tinson have been trying to sabotage a friend of mine's wedding. That ends now. If any of those three leave these premises for the rest of the day, they will be arrested. I am leaving Officer Clark here to monitor the departure of any guests from this property with orders to arrest any of those three individuals on sight. Is that understood?"

He glared at them until both the guard and Johnny Tinson nodded.

"Good. Now enjoy your wedding, like we intend to enjoy ours."

He walked over to me. "Care to give me a ride to the church?"

"Sure."

As I walked around to the driver's side, he added, "By the way, I kind of like this whole look you have going on. Very Warrior Princess."

(I'll leave out my reaction to that little comment. Good thing Matt doesn't take me seriously. He just laughed. Well, I always did say I wanted a man who'd ignore my anger but pay attention to my tears. Somehow I tend to forget that, though, when I'm angry.)

CHAPTER FORTY-ONE

We were the last ones to arrive at the church. All the guests were already there and seated. I quickly switched out of my shoes and lined up with exactly two minutes to spare.

Jamie grabbed my hand. "The decorations are gorgeous. Thank you."

"Thank my grandpa. And sorry they don't match the dresses."

"That's okay. It's all okay. I get to marry the man I love today and that is all that matters." She squeezed my hands, her eyes starting to tear.

The wedding march started.

I glanced into the church. Mason and my grandpa were at the front, waiting. The pews were full of guests. It was time.

I pointed to the two flower girls and gestured them towards the aisle. They were absolutely adorable twin second cousins of Jamie's, both five years old, wearing little pink frilly dresses and with bows in their hair. They tottered down the aisle, spilling white petals left and right.

Behind them came the ring bearer, a little boy in a tuxedo whose mom had to run up and help keep him on track when he suddenly stopped midway down the aisle and looked like he was going to cry.

And then the parade of bridesmaids started.

Jamie is a great person. Love her to death. But her third cousin who she hadn't spoken to in at least six months did not need to be a bridesmaid. Nor did her best friend from high school who was married with three kids and who she hadn't spoken to since number two was born.

But that was Jamie. She had to include everyone.

So we stood there and waited while eight bridesmaids and matching groomsmen walked down the aisle. Even though I was technically the maid of honor and Matt was not the best man, I walked down the aisle with him. Because if there was any man on this planet I was going to walk down any sort of aisle with, it was him. Mason's law school buddy Mitch, who was the best man, walked with Caroline and good riddance to them both.

By the time I reached the end all I wanted was for it to be over soon because I was not used to wearing heels anymore and I certainly was not used to wearing them while standing in front of a room full of important people.

But then it was Jamie's turn.

I almost cried. She was glowing with happiness. And so beautiful in that dress that Greta had given her. And her father looked so sad and proud at the same time. It was a perfect wedding moment.

And to see how Mason watched her as she walked towards him. When I saw one single tear slide down his cheek I had to look away so I wouldn't start bawling.

No matter what I might think of him, in that moment I knew he was the right choice for her. He might be uptight, but he'd shown time and time again how much he loved her. And that look in his eyes as he took her hand from her father?

Perfection.

My grandpa smiled at both of them and then turned his attention to the crowd. "Ladies and gentlemen, we are gathered here today to witness the joining of these two bright lives together."

The rest of the speech was short and sweet, but I wasn't really listening, I was just trying to keep it together so I wouldn't turn into a horrible, crying mess.

I almost made it, too, until Mason had to say his vows. And then the way his voice wavered as he promised to love my friend forever and his hand trembled as he put the ring on her finger? And the way Jamie started to sniffle? It was just too much.

Fortunately Jamie's mom was in the front row and armed with plenty of tissues. At that point I figured I'd done my duty and sank down next to her and sobbed while a woman with the most amazing voice sang a song about forever love.

When that was done, my grandpa stepped forward once more. "We have witnessed the joining of these two wonderful people. Now let us celebrate the new Mr. and Mrs. Mason Maxwell."

We all cheered as they walked down the aisle, beaming with happiness.

It was wonderful.

Maybe it wasn't what Jamie had planned down to the littlest detail, but all the parts that mattered had happened. Given the circumstances, I considered that more than an accomplishment, I considered it a miracle.

Now all that was left was to hope that Greta and Jean-Philippe would come through on the reception.

CHAPTER FORTY-TWO

As I waited for everyone to exit the church, I found myself cornered by Mason's grandmother. She's ninety-five years old and *seems* incredibly frail, but that woman…

She's fierce.

"You're next." She nodded with all the certainty of a woman who's always gotten her way for close to a century.

"Next to what?"

"Get married, dear. Mason tells me you and Matthew Barnes are an item."

"We've been dating, but I seriously doubt we'll get married anytime soon." I looked around for someone to rescue me, but no one was nearby.

"How old are you?" she demanded.

"Thirty-six."

"That's not young. I married Mason's grandpa when I was seventeen. You better get married soon."

I gritted my teeth. "And why's that?"

"The clock's ticking, young lady. If you don't get married soon, you won't have kids."

I was tempted to explain to her that kids can in fact be conceived outside of wedlock and that some women actually don't want kids at all, but decided I really didn't want to give Mason's grandma a heart attack on his wedding day.

Of course, me being me, I still had to say something. I settled for, "You know, they actually say forty is the new thirty."

"Not where your ovaries are concerned, young lady. Tick-tock."

How had I ended up in this conversation? And what business was it of hers if my ovaries were shriveling up and dying as we spoke? She wasn't family. Mine or Matt's. And yet, somehow we live in this world where random people can have an opinion—and voice it—about a woman's reproductive plans.

What the...

I looked around again, desperate for someone to save me and saw Matt leaning against the wall on the other side of the church grinning at me. That little...He knew. And he was leaving me to her. Like throwing the weaker lamb to the wolves.

"Speaking of Matthew Barnes, I better go grab him before someone else does, yeah?"

"Good thinking, dear. A catch like that, you better lock him down while you have the chance."

Right. Because men are these wayward creatures that will just blow away if they aren't nailed to the floor with wedding vows and babies.

I hurried away from her as fast as I could in three-inch heels.

"Did you get the 'you're next' talk?" Matt asked me.

"Yes. Why didn't you save me?"

"Because she would've probably forced me to propose to

you right here and now and I didn't want to hear you say no in front of a witness."

"With her as a witness I might've said yes. That woman is scary."

"Oh, if that's the case..." He grabbed my hand and took a step in her direction.

"Stop. That is not funny."

He tugged my hand gently, but then his phone started ringing. "I better take this."

While he answered the call I slipped out of my heels. I figured no one was watching me anymore and my tights would survive the barefoot walk to the reception area.

Lucky for me someone had come to lead Mason's grandma away but I wasn't going to chance running into her again by moving from that spot for at least another five minutes.

Matt hung up and glanced at me.

"What? Who was it?" I asked.

"Ben. He had good news. Of a sort."

"What's that?"

"Bobby and Johnny Tinson were just arrested trying to sneak away from the Kepper Ranch."

"Really? That's great news. Now we can have a reception without worrying about them doing something else stupid. Any chance they confessed?"

"Actually. Seems Bobby isn't as good as Johnny at keeping his mouth shut. He already said enough for Ben to tie them to the water damage to the church."

"What about Margaret? I know she had to be the one that hurt Elaine."

"Nope. Nothing on her. And she's still at the ranch."

"Wait...Ben was the only officer watching the ranch, right?"

"Right."

"And he just arrested Bobby and Johnny and I presume is bringing them in for holding?"

He nodded.

"So who's watching the ranch now?"

"No one."

I crossed my arms and glared at him. "Matt."

"What?"

"Who do you think is behind all this? Bobby Tinson? Do you really think he thought all of this up? No. It's Margaret Kepper. She's the only one with enough of a motive."

"Okay, so it's Margaret Kepper. I can agree with that."

"And your officer just drove off and left her alone to do whatever she's going to do."

"Where would she go? No one knows where the reception is."

"I wouldn't bet money on that. First, that SUV was seen at Greta's a few days ago. So they already suspect. And when I was at Jamie's I heard her mention it to the brides-maids. All it takes is one and since Caroline was there I wouldn't be surprised if she picked up the phone and called Margaret Kepper herself."

"We can't arrest her if she hasn't done anything, Maggie."

I glared him down trying to perform some sort of Vulcan mind control to sway him to my side. (Fancy's the master of that. She stares me down and suddenly I'm reaching for her treat bag as if it was my idea to give her just one more.)

It wasn't working, but then his phone rang again.

"Matt Barnes."

I watched intently as he said, "She is? What did she say?" And then "Uhuh. Okay. Well, pick her up."

He hung up.

"Well?"

"Elaine woke up. She never made any brownies at all. That must've all been Margaret. It seems Margaret came by last night for a final fitting on her dress and suggested they drink some champagne to celebrate. Elaine drank a couple of glasses and then started to feel ill so ran to the bathroom where she passed out. And Margaret just left her there. Next thing Elaine knew she was in the hospital."

"Got her!"

Matt gave me a long look.

"And I'm glad to hear Elaine is okay, too," I added.

His phone rang again. This time his end of the conversation was, "She's not? Well, find her."

"What now?"

"She isn't at the ranch. You were right. The security guard said she left right after Ben took Bobby and Johnny into custody."

"Then we better get to Greta's."

He glanced at my feet. "Barefoot?"

"My boots are in the foyer. Let's go." I ran down the aisle, dug out my boots, and sat on the ground to put them on.

"I'm driving," he said, twirling his keys as he waited for me.

"No. You drive too slow."

"Not in my police vehicle, which is parked right outside."

"I thought you were off duty."

"I am, but I figured with everything that had been happening better have it handy."

I flashed him a smile. "Even better. Lights and sirens. Let's go."

CHAPTER FORTY-THREE

WE MADE GOOD TIME GETTING TO BAKERSTOWN. IT WAS winter in Colorado and starting to get dark so we didn't make *that* good a time, but we definitely got there faster than we would've in my van. And Matt, thankfully, is actually willing to speed when he's in his cop role. (Other times he seems to think the speed limit is actually an upper limit. Crazy man.)

We were one curve in the road away from Greta's when I saw a fancy SUV pulled over to the side of the road and a small figure in a big snow coat climbing up the mountainside towards her house.

"Pull over," I shouted.

I jumped out the door before he even stopped and raced towards the figure on the hillside. I stopped at the edge of the road. "Margaret Kepper. Stop where you are. It's over."

She glanced at me just long enough for me to confirm it was her and then turned back to her uphill climb.

"Oh no you don't." I plowed into the snow—which was up to mid-calf and higher than my snow boots—and chased after her.

She tried to run away, but I wasn't having it. I dove at her, wrapping my arms around her thighs and took her down face-first into a snow bank.

It turns out I'm a fierce powderpuff player and that when we used to do midnight girls vs. guys "tackle" games I dominated. (Maybe because I was the only one actually trying to play tackle football while the other girls were coming up with clever plays like "everyone strip down to their bra so the boys are too distracted and we can score a touchdown.")

Anyway. I took her out. Sure, I could've just let Matt grab her, but she'd tried to ruin my best friend's wedding. I had feelings about that and they needed somewhere to go. Dive tackling the culprit into a snow bank seemed like a good use for them.

She tried to elbow me in the face, but I dodged it. "What is wrong with you? Seriously. Stop already."

"Jamie Green ruined my wedding. What did I ever do to her that she hates me so much?"

"Jamie doesn't hate you. I'm pretty sure she doesn't even know who you are."

That seemed to take all the wind out of her. She slumped into the ground and started to cry. "I planned my wedding a year in advance. And then she goes and changes her date last minute and everyone cancels on me so they can go to her wedding instead. Just like in high school."

"What'd she do to you in high school?"

"I was going to throw this big party at my dad's ranch and everyone was going to come and it was going to make me popular. But then Jamie suddenly hooks up with Dan and convinces him to throw a party at his ranch that same night. And no one came to my party. She ruined everything."

"I bet Elaine went to your party."

"Elaine doesn't count."

"Yeah, those friends that are always there for you no matter what, worthless aren't they? I mean who wants those when you can have the type of friends who cancel when something better comes along."

She stared at me, confused.

"Just in case you missed it, that was sarcasm. You don't deserve a friend like Elaine. And I hope she finally sees that now."

I stood up as Matt joined us. He eyed me up and down for a second. "You're going to need to change."

"Why?" I glanced down. "Oh. Right."

My tights were torn in at least three different spots and my knees were a little bloody. And somehow I'd managed to tear a huge section of the floofy little skirt on my dress so that it was less-than-decent now.

"Your hair, too."

I reached up to touch it. It was still sprayed into oblivion, but it seemed a whole section had come loose from its pins and was sticking out at an odd angle.

"Well, good thing I already know Greta has a dress that'll fit me then. And that she has about ten guest rooms. I'm sure one has a brush I can use. You mind driving me up to her place before you take this crazy woman in?"

"Oh I'm not taking her in." He pulled Margaret down the hill and locked her in the back of the vehicle. "I'll let Greta's security call someone who's actually on duty tonight." He pulled me close for a quick kiss. "This is New Year's Eve and I'm going to spend it with the woman I love, not filling out paperwork."

"Good man. Smart man." But if he proposed to me... We were going to have words.

CHAPTER FORTY-FOUR

NOT ONLY DID GRETA LET ME BORROW THE GORGEOUS blue dress but she also let me take a wonderfully hot shower to wash away the chill of burying myself in a snowbank while wearing a short dress. That also meant I could wash out all the hairspray and wear my hair loose and falling down my back, although I was likely to pull it into a sloppy bun before the night was out.

When I finally joined the party I found Matt and Greta waiting for me. Matt let out a low whistle. "Now that is a dress that works."

"I told her it is hers. It can be her something blue on her wedding day. Even if her wedding day is on the side of a mountain alone with the man she loves."

"Is that what you want?" he asked me.

"Can we just get through the rest of *this* wedding before we try to go there, please?"

Matt kissed my cheek. "As you wish."

"Greta, how's Jean-Philippe getting along?" I asked.

"See for yourself." She led me to the kitchen and I peeked inside.

Jean-Philippe was like I'd never seen him before. He's usually over-the-top dramatic or almost catatonically relaxed, but in the kitchen he was a man in his element. He was cutting something up, while tasting something else, and then turning to shout in French and English and who-knew-what other languages at the others who were preparing the food under his supervision.

It was organized chaos at its finest.

Greta eyed him appreciatively.

"Remember what you told me, Greta. Never marry a chef."

"I was not thinking of marrying him." She winked at me and took another step into the kitchen. In an odd way they were a good match.

I left them to it.

As I stepped into the main room I almost bumped into my grandpa who was loitering near the door. "How's Jean-Philippe?" he asked.

"Leave him be, Grandpa. If anyone needs to defend my honor at this point in time, it's Matt, not you." I hooked my arm through his and led him towards the nearest table. It was filled with a huge assortment of delicious-looking finger foods.

I snagged myself some sort of crostini appetizer that was positively decadent. Figs and foie gras with honey drizzled on top if I had to guess.

"Thank you again for everything you did today," I told him.

"You're welcome. Jamie's like another granddaughter to me. I was happy to help."

I nodded to where Lesley was talking to someone on the other side of the room. A ring flashed as she raised her left hand.

"So I take it you're telling everyone you're married now?"

He nodded. "We're ready to start our lives together."

I grabbed another bite of food—this one some sort of butter-soaked lobster bite—and swallowed it down so fast I almost didn't taste the buttery goodness.

"Grandpa? Is Lesley going to move in with you? With… us? Or are you going to move in with her? Or…?"

"Don't worry about it, Maggie. We'll figure that out next year."

But I did. And next year was only a few hours away.

Matt grabbed my hand and bowed over it like a gentleman. "My lady. May I have the pleasure of your company?"

"Of course."

I let him lead me around the room, sampling all the delicious food and talking to the other guests. It was so different to be at a wedding as part of a couple. It was…almost fun.

We ran into Greta again on the other side of the room, daintily eating a stuffed mushroom from a table that was clearly labeled as vegan.

"So Jean-Philippe did honor the guest's wishes, did he?" I asked. "He actually came through with some healthy foods for all of Jamie's friends?"

Greta laughed. "No. The man was too upset for that. I brought in a specialist."

"Ah. Smart woman. Just don't tell anyone they aren't eating food by the famed Jean-Philippe Gaston."

She smiled. "Their loss, no?"

I let Matt pull me into a slow dance before moving on to inspect the desserts. Jamie's cupcakes were center stage like some sort of display straight out of *Cupcake Wars*, but nearby there were also a series of small cakes that could easily serve another hundred guests as well as a large fresh fruit display and a chocolate fountain.

"Greta did well," I told Matt.

"So did you. You really pulled this together." He brushed a strand of hair behind my ear. "So, you want a wedding on the side of a mountain, do you?"

I must have looked as panicked as I felt, because he laughed and pulled me close. "Does the thought of spending forever with me really scare you that much?"

"No. It's just...It's too soon."

"Three months is too soon?"

"Yes. Definitely. It's all raging hormones at this point and no sense. I have flaws, Matt. I'm sure you do, too."

He chuckled. "So when is enough time?"

"Definitely not three months, that's for sure."

He took my chin in his hand and stared into my eyes. "But not three years either, Maggie."

"At least wait until spring, would you?"

"Done." He turned and started to walk away.

"What? No. Wait? I wasn't..."

He turned and winked at me. "Come on. Let's go congratulate the happy couple. And, I promise, no more talk of weddings for the rest of the night."

I hurried after him. "But that spring thing...I didn't really mean..."

He kissed me. "No more talk about it tonight. Let's just celebrate our friends' happiness and let tomorrow bring what it will."

The rest of that night was the best New Year's Eve I'd ever celebrated. Finally I was where I wanted to be, surrounded by friends, family, and a man I loved. Not to mention I'd been instrumental in pulling off an awesome party and getting a crazy, psycho person locked away.

Not bad. Not bad at all.

The adventures continue in A Poisoned Past and Puppermints.

ABOUT THE AUTHOR

When Aleksa Baxter decided to write what she loves it was a no-brainer to write a cozy mystery set in the mountains of Colorado where she grew up and starring a Newfie, Miss Fancypants, that is very much like her own Newfie, in both the good ways and the bad.

You can reach her at aleksabaxterwriter@gmail.com or on her website aleksabaxter.com.

To hear about new releases or promotions, sign up for her mailing list.